# A Box of Chocolates

by
Bryan Mooney

(A book of award winning short stories & excerpts from current and upcoming books.)

Copyright© January 2014 by BME

Published worldwide by BME - all rights reserved.

Printed in the United States of America and protected under all applicable copyright protections.

All rights reserved.

This book, or parts thereof, may not be reproduced in any form without the express written permission from the publisher BME.
Published simultaneously in Canada, UK, India, Mexico, France, Brazil, Denmark, Italy, Spain, Japan, Canada, and other countries worldwide.

This book is a work of fiction. Any references to historical events, real people, or real places are used fictitiously. Other names, characters, places, and events are products of the author's imagination and any resemblance to actual events, regions, places, or persons living or dead is entirely coincidental.

# Novels by Bryan Mooney

A Box of Chocolates

Love Letters

The POTUS Papers

A Second Chance

INDIE—A Female Vigilante

*All books available wherever fine books are sold.*

*"Books are like a box of chocolates,
you never know what you're gonna find."
An assortment of readings, short stories, and excerpts
from current and upcoming works by Bryan Mooney!
—Enjoy*

*Dedicated to
my loving wife
Bonnie*

# Acknowledgements

I want to thank BME publishing for their unwavering support of my writing over the years and allowing me to travel in uncharted waters and my heartfelt thanks to Nicholas Patterson and my publisher at BME, James Sparks.

My sincerest thanks to Maria Karamitsos for her special assistance in helping me with my Greek throughout my books. I know I can always count on her generous support. *Epharistos Maria*!

In addition, I would be remiss in not thanking my wonderful friends at Aberdeen who are always there to help me, read my work, and offer their kind encouragement and support. Thank you all.

—BDM

# Contents

Charley
Driving to Kingdom Come
I Met Someone
The Beautiful Redhead
The Mountain
Mail-Order Bride
Things My Mother Told Me
The Painter from Syros
Yes, Officer
Jig
What a Woman Says
Mighty Miss
Love Letters
The Negotiator
A New Beginning
Fitz
The Perfect Baby
Excuses
Have a Heart
Words
The Lemon Trees
Turnin' 30
Danny Dark
INDIE—A Female Vigilante
Diana Margarita
A Second Chance
Dog with No Name
My Extraordinary Night with Frank
Breakfast

# Charley

It was summertime, a time of hot afternoons and cool breezes. It was a time of homemade apple pies, state fairs, and fresh watermelons. It was a time for picnics. We loved to spread out our blanket on a grassy hillside with our wine and cheese while we watched the sailboats glide by on the lake far below us. My love and I lay beneath the shade of a tall majestic oak tree as it opened its cool comforting umbrella, and we counted the pillow-soft clouds drifting by above us.

"I love you," she told me.

I stroked her hair as her head lay in my lap. "I love you too," I said, my lips touching hers, once, twice, and then a third time. It was perfect. We were together, and nothing would ever come between us... but that was before Charley. It was Charley with a Y.

Life was good before Charley came bounding into our life one dog-day July afternoon, so small yet so large. Not that it was not good once Charley was with us ... it was just different.

Charley lived with us from the time we woke up in the morning until the time we went to sleep at night. We would lie in bed so close to one another, and Charley was there between us. I would touch her back and kiss her neck. My hand would slide to her waist—and Charley was there. My sweet would whisper a story to cheer me up or calm me down, but she knew Charley was always with us. She was distressed. Her hair, once soft as a wandering wind, was now brittle as a nest of twigs.

Over time, we began to describe our life as before Charley and after Charley, we code-named it BC and AC, as if Charley could understand what we were saying. However, we made room for Charley in our life. We had no choice.

As Charley grew larger, we treated him the way the experts told us. We soon knew it was time to do something, but we waited too long. Charley viciously attacked her, and as I rushed her to the hospital we made a decision ... it was time for Charley to go.

The blood drained from her face.

"Everything will be okay," I told her, as I held her hand while we waited.

"I'm scared," she said in a hollow tone, her once-determined will and strong hands now weak like putty.

I gripped her hand tighter. "It will all work out," I told her, kissing her forehead, but I was afraid. I was afraid for her, for me ... for us.

She looked through my facade and smiled, "I love your aftershave ... it smells of salt air."

"I love you," I said, holding back my tears as the white-coated doctors and flowered-covered nurses took her away. I was more scared then I have ever been in my entire life. Hours later, she returned to me, her face drawn.

My face questioned her.

She knew me. "Charley's gone," she said in a tired sigh.

I stayed with her all night, then the next and the next.

Last summer we celebrated five years with a picnic by the river, she in her pink dress and I with my pink ribbon. We were both happy that Charley was gone... at least so they say. I never believed them, but I can say that the wine seemed to taste so much sweeter that year and the year after that. One day at a time, we would always say, and every day I would whisper and pray: *Stay away Charley, just stay away.*

# Driving to Kingdom Come

I could see my sister was nervous as her fingers gripped the steering wheel of the car. She gripped it so tight her knuckles had turned white, drained of blood. She tapped her thumb on the wheel, a nervous habit. She looked at me and smiled weakly to show that everything was all right. A car full of police guards passed us on the empty streets of the desert capitol. We saw no brake lights flash and now had only six more blocks to go.

This was the first time I had accompanied my sister on a freedom drive, but now both of us were having second thoughts about this adventure. Sixty women had volunteered to protest the female driving ban in the Kingdom by driving themselves that night without a male family member or hired male driver, a routine everyday occurrence practiced by women elsewhere worldwide.

We reached the main square. I noticed a white sedan sitting off to the side of the road with its parking lights on. Three more blocks to go, and then we would be safe.

The parked car eased out onto the street behind us and turned on its blue flashing lights indicating they wanted us to pull over. It was the religious police or rather the *Committee for the Promotion of Virtue and Prevention of Vice,* as they were officially known.

What was my sister's infraction? Driving the car herself, late at night, without a male escort and not wearing the traditional attire expected in the Kingdom. She did not wear the long, stifling hot *abaya* frock or even her *shemagh* headdress. I was only twelve and had not yet experienced the *hayz* so I was exempt from the dress rules because I was not yet considered a woman.

She sat straight in the driver's seat waiting for her interrogation to begin. Her hands clenched the wheel even tighter. Beads of perspiration formed on the back of her knuckles, drops of sweat dripped onto her jeans.

Four men converged on the car at the same time yelling and shouting at us. They hit the side of the car, the windshield, and the roof with their long wooden sticks. My sister had warned me as to what to expect should the religious police stop us. *Whatever you do, remain calm,* she warned me.

Finally, a senior-looking official with a long white beard approached the SUV, and the others moved to the side to allow him passage. He motioned for her to roll down the window.

She pressed the power window button, then handed him her international driver's license through the opening.

He examined it and shoved it back at her in disdain. "What are you doing? You know it is against the law for women to drive here in the Kingdom. And look at you and your state of undress. You are old enough to know that you could excite men here in the Kingdom with what you are wearing."

I glanced at my sister's casual attire of t-shirt, jeans and sandals. Very provocative I thought to myself, smiling.

"And what are you laughing at young one?" He yelled in my direction. "See," he said to the other men standing around the car, "not only does she flaunt our laws but corrupts our youth with her behavior and dress."

"It is not illegal for a woman to drive a vehicle in the Kingdom," she said calmly.

"Yes, it is," he stammered, taken aback at her temerity.

"Show me the law," she asked, her voice rising in pitch.

He stuttered and stammered. "And…and our learned clerics have told us that women who drive could damage their ovaries and give birth to deformed children. Is that what you are trying to do, break another law and harm your ovaries? You should be ashamed of yourself and the example you are setting for this young one."

"Give me a break. You don't know what the hell you are talking about."

"Blasphemer!" he shouted and stepped back away from the car.

I reached over and squeezed my sister's leg reminding her of the caution she had given me earlier. Her mouth suddenly clenched shut, and she looked straight ahead. She got the message; hopefully it was not too late.

He shoved his head deep inside the car stopping mere inches from my sister's face and whispered, "Are you an outside agitator? Are you a blasphemer?" The world became silent. It was a serious accusation, one of the most serious one could make against a man in the Kingdom much less to a woman.

I saw her swallow and turn her head towards him her fingers on the steering wheel now tightened, "No. I am not a blasphemer."

"Are you an outside agitator?" He asked slowly in an ominous tone. Everyone knew the penalty for agitators in the Kingdom.

"No, I am from here in the Kingdom," she tried to say calmly, her voice shaking. Their eyes locked on one another and the struggle for dominance dragged on for what seemed like hours when in fact it was mere seconds.

Finally, she looked away, and my sister said, "I am the daughter of the family of El Shahid, and this is my sister visiting from America. We are on our way home. Our driver… was… taken ill, and my father and brother were not available to drive us. We would like to leave now to go home."

His eyes never left her face. He did not say a word. "Let them go," he finally shouted to the other men. "We have much work to do tonight here in the Kingdom." Turning back to my sister he whispered, "Tell El Shahid that I will come for a visit… soon. Now go to your father's house where you belong."

We drove home in silence since the encounter on the street left us both shaken. Neither one of us said a word until we reached home and hugged each other tight.

When I returned to America, my sister joined me, and many times we laughed about what happened that night on a downtown deserted city street, but both of us knew what could have happened. I think of that night some eight years later as my sister drives me to her swearing in ceremony to be the first female junior congresswoman from our great state. We have not been back to the Kingdom, and we may never return to our righteous homeland. But then again, maybe it is time for change?

# I Met Someone

"I met someone, Mom," Brad said, ever so quietly, looking down at the floor of the restaurant, with his mop head of gorgeous blond hair covering his face. He had inherited his tangled blond hair, that looked like it had never been combed, and his dusty blue eyes from his father's side of the family. Brad Silver looked more like a surfer from California, than a Vermont Mountain Man. He had broad shoulders and strong coarse hands, the result of years of hard work tending to the trees at the family's maple farm.

Brad and his mother Jane had driven in from their farm outside of Rutland, about thirty miles away, to visit the nearby town of Woodstock, Vermont. They were running errands, like most of the people that day in this mountain town on this, crisp November morning.

The town of Woodstock, population of two thousand, is a quaint small town, in the lush green mountains of Vermont. It has two main streets, Central and Elm, and at their intersection lies the heart of the village. At the town center is the local hardware store, Maguire's, standing beside Doc's pharmacy and across the street from Bentleys, the local eatery.

Brad and his mom settled into a booth at Bentleys to enjoy a quiet lunch... and to talk.

He continued, telling his mother, who was intent on listening to his every word, "I am really crazy about her, and it is driving me nuts." His mother was always happy to have her youngest and now her only son share things with her, but what he was saying now was a little unsettling. She wanted to be happy for her young son, but she was not sure of what was coming next.

Her son Brad, even as a boy, had always been the quiet one. He was the one you could count on. He was the one everyone went to for help. Brad did not open up to many people. Not even to his mother. Now he was sharing something very private with her, but a strange sense of dread shivered through her body. In her heart, she knew what was coming.

He had spent most of the recent summer, the slow season for maple farmers, in Florida, taking some college courses, but when he returned there was something different about him. Unsettled. His mother tried to get him to talk about it since his return home but to no avail. She knew it was only a matter of time, and it seemed that now was that time.

"Do I know her?" she asked quietly.

"No," he said without looking up.

"What's her name, Brad?"

The sparkle came back to his dusty blue eyes, when he looked up and said, "Kasey, mom, Kasey Morgan. She's a marine biologist." His whole demeanor had changed. He was smiling from ear to ear.

Seeing him this animated reminded her of the time Brad and his older brother Jack had gone fishing together at the Rutland Dam. They had caught many fish, but then somehow managed to slide into the muddy pond that had formed behind the small earthen dam. They were both covered with mud when they came home; she hardly recognized them as her sons.

Their laughter and the smiles on their faces made it hard to scold them for getting so muddy. She was just happy to see her two boys, safe and playing together, again. That was before her son Jack had gone into the Marine Corps.

"Is she from around here?" She asked, happy to see him so animated.

Mary, a longtime fixture at Bentleys, bringing them their lunch, delayed his response.

Bentleys was a local institution in Woodstock. During the day, it had a sandwich crowd for lunch, and at night, you could have a good home-cooked meal there. The place was crowded until its midnight closing time.

After Mary delivered their lunch, he slowly looked up at his mother as he continued telling her about the girl he had met while in Florida.

"No, she's not from around here. She's originally from New Orleans but now lives in Fort Lauderdale," he said, as he lowered his head, to concentrate on his sandwich.

Jane felt a sense of unknown dread, a feeling that every mother feels at certain times in their lives, and this was one of them. She felt it travel from her heart, to her stomach, and it just lay there, slowly tying a knot in her gut. She had a feeling that she knew where this was going. She also knew that she did not want to lose another son.

He managed a small smile as he said, "Mom, she is so cute and so smart. She has a great sense of humor and a very dry wit. You'll love her. She reminds me a lot of you."

"How did you meet her?" she asked trying to remain calm and interested.

"We met when I was going to some summer school classes in Florida this summer. One day they cancelled my class at the last minute, and I wandered into a lecture hall after seeing the sign that said it was about *Saving the Everglades*. Kasey was a guest lecturer that day, and I fell for her really hard." He grinned, obviously thinking back to that day.

"After the lecture, I was trying to come up with a way to meet her, and next thing I know she was standing in front of me. Mom, she is tall like you, with the prettiest green eyes and a gorgeous figure. She makes me laugh."

His mother picked at the salad in front of her.

"Kasey had a stern look on her face when she looked at me and said, 'Do you always come into a classroom late?' She had both hands on her hips." He paused.

"She said it with such a straight face. I didn't know what to say. Then she broke out laughing. Kasey told me she was not a professor but worked for the Florida Wildlife Federation and was just helping out as a guest lecturer.

"She introduced herself and then asked me if I wanted to go to the beach that night, at sunset. I started thinking, on the beach, at night with the moonlight and with her. Are you kidding? 'Of course,' I told her, 'sure I would love to go.'

"That night we met by the beach in Boca Raton and walked over the dunes to the ocean. I could hear the waves breaking on the beach. It was so romantic. Then she handed me a flashlight and clipboard. I found out she had volunteered me to help conduct a census count of the loggerhead sea turtles with her and some others from the foundation. After that night, we saw each other just about every day. We hit it off great. I really liked her... a lot."

"You never mentioned her when you called this summer," Jane Silver said, as she ordered another coffee from Mary.

"I didn't know where the relationship was going and thought that she was just another girl that I liked to go out with and have fun. And besides I didn't want to send Dad off the deep end." He smiled.

"At the end of August, she went back to New Orleans to visit her folks for two weeks and I figured that was probably the end of it. I was planning on breaking it off when she came back to Florida because I knew I would be coming home to Vermont soon. But, Mom, I nearly went crazy counting the days until she returned." His mother smiled a wistful smile as she drank her coffee.

"When she came back, I couldn't keep my hands off of her and was relieved to find out that she felt the same way. When we got back to her place I nearly tore her clothes off and…"

"Brad, dear, you can spare me all of the details of your joyous reunion."

"Sorry, Mom. A few weeks later though we broke it off when I came home to Vermont with both of us feeling miserable but knowing it just wouldn't work out. But she called me last week, and I knew I had to be with her."

"What are you going to do?"

"I don't know, Mom. I just don't know. I don't want to disappoint you and Dad, and now with Jack gone, it's just the three of us. I try to help Dad with the farm, but you know that I was never the businessman in the family. That was Jack's love and strength. I was always the tree hugger, remember."

"Have you told your father?"

"No. I haven't said anything to him. I wanted to talk with you first."

"You need to. He's hurting Brad, and he still thinks that Jack's leaving was partially his fault, that maybe if they had gotten along better he would still be here, alive. Why don't you tell him when we get home?"

He nodded as his gaze wandered off in the distance.

The town of Woodstock was like a little piece of colonial history. This quaint, small town had narrow streets with restored buildings, and two traffic lights. Between the hectic tourist seasons, life slowed down to a crawl, just the way everyone liked it.

Jane paid for their lunch, and they headed down the small main street to Doc's Pharmacy on Central Avenue. They stopped at Doc's to pick up some pills for Brad's aging golden retriever, Sammy, who had come down with an autumn cough. Old age was tough on a dog.

Jane and Brad Silver, walking down the main street of Woodstock, made a striking pair as mother and son. Jane Silver was over six feet tall with long black hair, and only slight streaks of grey, even though she was well over sixty years old. Brad Silver was slightly taller than his statuesque mother, with broad shoulders and a cheerful but quiet disposition.

Everyone who passed them said hello. Everybody liked Jane, but all the local girls loved Brad. He had a certain boyish charm, even at the ripe old age of twenty-eight but his father, Hal Silver, had not been into town in years, at least not since his son Jack had died. Hal always said he did not need anything. He had the farm, and that was all he wanted.

After leaving Doc's, they both went off in opposite directions. Brad had some of his own errands to run, and they agreed to meet again later at three o'clock back at the truck.

When Jane Silver next saw her strapping young son walking down Main Street, she could not help but notice something very different about him, Brad had gotten a haircut. She chuckled to herself as they walked back to the truck.

She knew he was getting ready to leave Vermont, and his life here, behind him. She was determined to make however long she had left with him the most memory-filled and unforgettable time of their life. But she was torn. She loved him dearly, and while she wanted him to be happy, she would have preferred that he stay right here in Vermont. Either way she wanted to make sure that she was going to see her future grandkids.

As he approached her, he smiled that broad grin of his, and she tousled his hair and said, "Nice haircut, kiddo."

They headed back to the farm driving towards Rutland. The road was a scenic one, along the two-lane winding Route 4, with the mountains ahead of and beside them. You could look straight ahead and all around you see the wonderfully calming Vermont Mountains. The tall sentinels were shedding their summer green coats and putting on a beautiful array of fall colors with red, yellow, orange, and amber, autumn in New England in all its glory.

She drove the country road past the wide, fast-moving, shallow streams, popular with the fly-fishing crowd. The streams rambling beside the road acted as a traveling companion running all along Route 4 from Woodstock past Rutland all the way south to White River Junction. They passed a covered bridge, which straddled the fast-moving stream beneath it with its faded red coat badly needing repainting.

*Life in Vermont was wonderful or had been wonderful up until this point in time,* she thought wistfully. Glancing at Brad, she could not help but think how much he looked like his older brother. "Today you remind me so much your brother Jack and of your grandfather," she said to him in a wondrous sort of way.

Jack was the one with the business head on his shoulders, but he and his father just never saw eye to eye. After an entire day of arguing with his father about computerizing the inventory system, Jack said he had enough. He enlisted the next day in the Marine Corps to assert his independence. He went to his basic training in the Carolinas and looked so sharp in his uniform when he came home to visit. All the local girls fell in love with him. He finished the rest of his training and was sent overseas to the war zone. He didn't survive long. He was there only six months before he was killed in an enemy attack. Now she knew in her heart that she was going to lose another son.

Brad loved everything about Vermont. He looked out of the window of the old blue pickup truck and knew he would miss it.

Family was his blood, but the mountains, they got in your blood. He loved the cold winters with the howling winds and mountains of snow with the maple sap flowing into buckets of plenty followed by trout fishing in the rising streams and bountiful wildflowers greeting spring. He had always loved it here, but now he had found a new love…Kasey.

They approached the small gravel driveway in silence each lost in their own thoughts and as they drove past the sign for the turnoff that read *Silver Maple Farm*, she asked him softly, "When do you leave Brad?"

"In three weeks. Mom, I hope you don't mind, but I invited Kasey to stay with us and have Thanksgiving dinner with us. She said she would love to meet you and Dad. We leave the next day to go back to Florida." A wayward snowflake landed on the old truck's windshield.

---

When Hal Silver pulled his ten-year-old SUV into the snow-covered driveway, it was well past midnight. He was surprised to see the light on in their bedroom. It was located at the near the rear of the house, overlooking the tree line. He closed the car door and headed towards the old farmhouse. *Jane must still be awake, probably reading.* A wet snowflake brushed his cheek.

His regular Saturday night poker game finished late that night. He played with the same group of friends he had been playing with for over fifteen years. He had won again, not much, but the weekly poker game was a welcome relief from his everyday routine at their maple farm.

After parking the SUV he hobbled up the creaking back steps, nearly tripping over his walking cane. He found Jane still awake and reading her latest Danielle Steele romance novel. "Hi honey," he said as he leaned over to kiss her and started to get undressed for bed. "It's snowing," he commented.

"Ummh," she grunted. It was going to be another long winter. "Did you win tonight?" she asked casually.

"Yes, about thirty dollars."

"We need to talk," said Jane, sipping on her usual late night, maple cocoa. She closed her Danielle Steele paperback and fluffed up her pillows to make herself comfortable.

"That sounds ominous," Hal said from the bathroom over the noise of his electric toothbrush. "I'll be right in."

He came into the bedroom, took a sip from her cocoa, glided under the covers, and kissed her on the check.

She came right to the point, as was her way. "Brad has met a girl that he is really sweet on, and he's moving to Florida to be with her," she said softly.

"What? When did all of this happen?" he asked in astonishment, as he sat up in bed, all illusions of a peaceful night's sleep now vanquished with one sentence.

"He met her over the summer, when he was in Florida."

"And we're just hearing about it? How can he leave us now… the season starts in a couple of months?" Hal proclaimed, showing his anger and annoyance. "Is he still up? I wanna to talk to him," he asked as he rose from the bed, putting on his robe heading for the bedroom door.

"No, he's asleep. He waited up as late as he could for you, but he was up very early this morning and was dead tired."

"I can't believe this," muttered Hal pacing about the room, his usual practice when he was trying to sort out the answer to a particularly difficult problem.

"Come here." She patted the bed and motioned for him to join her. "Come back to bed, please. Let's talk."

His response was more of a snort than intelligible English, but she understood him as he sat down next to her.

"He's in love," she continued, "and whether anything comes of it remains to be seen, hopefully yes, but they are both young. Either way he is leaving here in a few weeks. We can either make this the best time or the most miserable time of our life and his life. The choice is ours. I, for one, would like to have Brad look back at this time before he leaves as good times with some very happy memories. I would also like to hold my grandchild, sooner rather than later."

"She's pregnant?" he shouted, as he sat up in bed, looking at her. "Is that what this is all about?"

"No, she's not pregnant. All I am saying is that if we push him away, it may be a long time before we see him again. I love you, and I love this farm, but we are not getting any younger, and there are still some places that I would like to see. I would love to leave this beautiful, snowy wonderland one winter and take a nice, long, two-week Caribbean cruise, in the warm tropical sun, with cold pina coladas and hot calypso dancing. That's what I would like to do."

"Leave it to you to get all goo-goo eyed when he mentions he loves somebody. Jane, this isn't some Danielle Steele romance novel. I have a living to make, a family to support, and this maple farm to run, and I was counting on his help to do it. What am I going to do now?"

She continued, "Maybe after three generations, it's time for another family to take a crack at this wonderful farm. We don't need the money. Besides you've had many offers to buy this farm over the years, and we've always said that family comes first… Well now, let's put that into action. But those are just my feelings. Think about it, and try to get some rest. Oh and by the way, she's joining us for Thanksgiving."

"What?"

"Goodnight dear." She kissed him on the cheek and turned out the light on the old wooden bed-stand.

*Thanksgiving!* Hal thought to himself, *that was it*. That's how she summed it up, nice neat, and tidy. Say goodbye to Brad, sell the farm that's been in the family for generations, and move to Florida and drink pina coladas. *Yeah, right*. He had a farm to run and a family to support; he couldn't be so carefree. How the hell was he going to do it? The hell with it! He didn't need anybody's help as he looked at his old, wooden cane leaning in the corner. He rolled over and tried to fall asleep; sleep, he knew now, would be a long time in coming.

Young Brad Silver wondered how his father would react when he told him the news that he was leaving. He hated to leave him now with the sugar sap season just three months away, but he really had no choice, he was starting his new job at the foundation on the Monday after he returned to Florida. How was Dad going to manage without his help? His mom and dad always told him to follow his heart, but he never knew it was going to be this difficult of a decision.

At sunrise, he rose to greet a new day and went downstairs to face the family. His dad was already gone, probably in the garage getting ready for the day's chores. Brad poured a cup of coffee and sweetened it with some maple sugar. He felt his mother's warm hand on his neck behind him, as she wished him a good morning. She grilled bacon, made some eggs, and potatoes and poured more coffee before sitting across from her son.

"Your father was a little upset last night when I spoke to him, so go easy on him."

"You told him?"

"Yes, I think he may come around, like always. On the bright side, I like your new haircut. It is very becoming on you," she said with a teasing smile. He laughed.

Once he finished his breakfast, and after wrestling on his heavy winter coat, Brad grabbed two large coffee mugs, one for him and one for his dad. Today they were going to survey the north section of the tree farm and check on the current condition of some of the oldest trees.

Brad gave his father the hot coffee and started loading up the all-terrain-vehicles (ATVs). His father, kneeling on the grounded tying up the ropes, looked at him and slowly smiled and said, "Thanks for the coffee. Time to get to work, son."

Hal Silver seemed to take the news better than Brad had thought he would. Maybe he was just too tired to fight it. Brad had thought that his dad would yell and try to talk him out of it, and he had dreaded telling him. *People fool you sometimes.*

The farm's huge maple-processing "hut" stood behind the farmhouse near the edge of the tree line near the garage. A light coat of snow the night before had dusted the ground like powered sugar, giving everything that white pre-holiday glow.

They loaded up their ATVs with ropes, saws, walkie-talkies, GPS and sampling devices, and log registers and headed for what they called the outback portion of the farm. They were going to inspect their largest and most productive trees. It took them over an hour until they made their first stop.

The Silver Maple Farm had been in the Silver family for many decades and was one of the largest sugar maple farms in the northeast, encompassing over 1,200 acres. Their trees produced the most sought after Grade-A, light amber maple sap, treasured by bakers and retail stores. The light amber sap took the shortest amount of time to boil off the accumulated water and had the highest and purest sugar content. It also had the perfect consistency for making maple syrup. It was a Silver Maple Farm specialty.

Maple trees begin storing their sugar supply during the fall and start to sap during early February through the end of April, their busiest part of their season. But the back-breaking season was preceded by months of testing and preparation. It was grueling work, and the timing as to when to tap the sugary trees had to be nearly flawless. Life on a maple farm was hard work.

Brad always remembered how his dad had first showed him how to draw sap from a tree. The tree is first drilled, and then a tap is installed in the sap hole. Then either a bucket or a sap line is attached to the spigot. Hal hired additional help over the years during the busy period, using local boys looking to make some extra money. They worked hard lugging buckets of sugary sap back and forth to the sugar shacks for processing, but the local boys still made time to ski the renowned slopes of Killington, Stratton, and other nearby world-class ski resorts.

Brad had done this work with his father for as long as he could remember. Sometimes the snow was so deep it would have to be shoveled out of the way to a tree just to tap into one.

The larger trees, over sixteen inches in diameter, could accommodate two spigots, one on each side of the tree. This doubled production once the trees were of the right age and dimension. Brad knew all of this and knew he would miss it. Today they were going to check on the old granddads. These were the oldest and largest of their trees, and were the most productive ones.

When her two men left for the day Jane Silver took the red SUV and headed into the nearby town of Rutland, to buy some supplies for Thanksgiving to send her son off with a bang.

Brad and his dad went to the most northern section and started their measurements. The narrow single-lane trail was just wide enough for a single vehicle and not much more. During the spring thaw, the muddy trials became quicksand-like and were treacherous to traverse in anything other than the ATVs.

The trees were like the mountains here, rising majestically on all sides tall and straight, all around as far as the eye could see. The trees ruled their world here. This was their domain, and they were unforgiving. A few years earlier his dad had been drinking heavily for weeks after Jack died and was alone in the woods one night trying to make some sense of the tragedy. Alone with an axe. A tree fell on him narrowly missing his skull but crushing his leg and hip. Now he needed a cane to get around the farm. The mountains showed mercy to no one.

"The trees look fine," his dad said aloud.

"Yeah," Brad responded as he leaped out of his vehicle and plodded over to examine one of their largest and most productive trees. It was one of his favorites. "It feels like this one is almost ready now," Brad said aloud, gently probing the bark.

"That's not good. It's way too early. Better go ahead and test it, Brad." His father frowned.

Brad pulled out a small V-shaped tool that he inserted ever so gently into the side of the old grandfather maple. He pulled out his timer stopwatch and clicked it on. The clicking on the stopwatch sounded like a heartbeat in the quiet forest. Tick, tick, tick. He could hear the watch as the seconds and then minutes ticked away. Nothing. Minutes more passed. Still nothing—no sap was flowing. That was a good thing.

A snowflake landed on Brad's cheek, then another and another. In the quiet peace of the forest, he thought of Kasey. He wondered what she was doing at that moment. Was she at work? He couldn't wait to see her again. His father's slow, deep voice in the woods interrupted his thoughtful silence. "Your mother told me about your girl in Florida. Maybe she'd like to live here in beautiful Vermont."

Brad looked away from the towering tree. "Dad, she's a marine biologist. That's what she does. She got me a job working with her at the foundation, where I can use some of my college courses."

"This place won't be the same without you. I know it has been tough on you here since your brother died, but I don't know what I'll do with you gone. First your brother now you... leaving us."

Hal looked away from his son and silently gazed back in the direction of the farmhouse. "But you have to do what is right for you. Jack and I butted heads all of the time about the business and ..." The snow was falling faster. It was now harder to see the top of the mountain.

"Jack wanted to computerize everything," he continued dusting it off his face, "and I bucked him every step of the way. I didn't want anything to change, and Jack wanted things to change yesterday. He got frustrated, struck out on his own, and joined the Marine Corps. I always felt guilty; like it was my fault he was killed. I took out my feelings of loss about Jack on you. That's not right, I can see that now, and I'm sorry."

Brad looked at his dad. He saw his tall, proud, and aging father in a completely new light. "I love you, Dad." They stood there looking at each other, in the quiet each understood the meaning of loss and redemption.

"Go check that spigot, son."

After fifteen minutes, Brad said, relief obvious in his voice, "It's okay." Sap this premature in the season would be disastrous. "There is nothing coming out, Dad." Brad stood up as the light snow, which had started swirling down through the canopy of trees, grew heavier.

"Your mom says she's coming for Thanksgiving."

"Yeah, Dad. Her name is Kasey. You're going to like her."

"I can't wait to meet her. We'll work this thing out, son, somehow. Come on, let's go see the old trees." They checked over sixty trees that day. The sap was still slumbering.

The snow was heavier as they made their way back to the farmhouse. "Right about now a hot shower and some warm maple rum would go down good," Hal joked to his son. His mind wandered. He liked things just the way they are.

Things were changing too rapidly. Maybe Brad will go to Florida and miss the farm. Maybe they won't hit it off, or maybe she'll love Vermont. What's not to love? He would show her the best hospitality that Vermont has to offer. Yes, that's exactly what he would do! She'll love it here. Maybe she'll move here... Don't kid yourself, old man.

As they were heading home to the farmhouse, Hal pulled over to the side of the trail, near their largest holly trees. He motioned Brad to join him. They proceeded to cut branches off the majestic berry-filled holly trees that were interspersed among the maples.

"Your mom can use these as holiday decorations at home," proclaimed Hal. "It is just the thing for the festive spirit." They loaded the branches into the snow-covered ATVs, and headed back to the farmhouse. This was the first time in years that Brad's father had suggested holiday decorations.

---

The Silver Maple farm consisted of the house for the family, which was a three-story building, with a slanted copper roof. The copper reflected the heat so that the heavy northeastern snow would slide off easier. Attached to the house was a lodge built to accommodate the seasonal workers and a processing building called the "sugar shack." The lodge could accommodate over twenty-plus workers during the peak time at the farm.

The kitchen in the farmhouse and lodge was made for cooking for large groups of hungry men, who worked harvesting the sugar sap. The two stoves in the kitchen had ten burners each, and just off the kitchen were two large dining rooms that could feed over twenty-five people at a time.

When Brad and his dad returned home the farm was in turmoil. Jane had hired two other women to help clean the house, as if they were getting ready for a wedding or a visit by royalty. All three were busy cleaning.

"What's going on here?" asked Hal.

The drapes were off the windows scattered about the floor, the carpets rolled back out of the way, and the floors had been scrubbed and polished to a high shine. They had cleaned all the mirrors and tables and everything was starting to look new, just the way Jane wanted.

"Don't stand in our way; we got lots of work to do!" thundered Jane. "The maple ham is in the oven and will be done in a half hour. Go upstairs and wash up. Dinner will be ready shortly. Heat me up some maple brandy. I feel like a party," said the exuberant Jane Silver as she danced to the Christmas music playing in the background. And party they did. Hal was beginning to get into the spirit and actually began to enjoy himself. He even laughed at her antics.

On Sunday, they had announced to everyone for miles around that they were having an open house. It was an open invitation until Brad left after Thanksgiving for friends, classmates, neighbors, and other townspeople who wanted to stop by and wish Brad well in his journey to Florida.

Jane and her crew cooked meals for the family and whoever came by for a visit at the Silver Farm. Holiday music blared nonstop while people came by to wish Brad and the Silver family well. There were normally ten to fifteen cars parked in the driveway, with more and more cars and trucks coming every day.

True to her word, Jane was going to make this a time to remember for her son Brad. She and Hal had made peace with each other and with the fact that Brad was leaving. Hal never disclosed his plan to convince Kasey to move to Vermont. Some things were better left unsaid.

They had so many people come to their house to celebrate, eat, drink, sing, and dance that Jane and Hal had invitations to over eight other holiday parties. That had never happened to them before. Since Hal's accident, they kept pretty much to themselves and stopped visiting neighbors and old friends.

Two days before Thanksgiving, Hal and Jane snuggled close together with their maple brandies in front of the dying bonfire at the back of the house, each in their own private worlds. A large snowflake drifted down to their laps, then another. They kissed before heading back into the warmth of the farmhouse. There was a big snowstorm coming in and heading their way.

The snow began to fall shortly after midnight and continued throughout the day. Hal loaded the huge fireplace with seasoned oak logs to maintain his roaring fire while a steady stream of visitors braved the early-season snowstorm and stopped by for some of the finest home cooking in Vermont. It was a joyous celebration—Thanksgiving was finally here. Jane dressed in her Sunday finest to make a good impression on her future daughter-in-law.

Jane saw Brad slumped in a chair by himself. "Her flight was rerouted to Detroit because of the snowstorm," Brad said glumly.

Jane hugged her son to cheer him up and make his blues go away. She lifted his chin. "Don't worry Brad. She'll be here. I just know she will." She grabbed him by the hand, "Come on, the guys are watching the football game in the back room."

He managed a weak smile.

During the game, he received a text: "LEAVING COLUMBUS FOR BALTIMORE. SEE YA SOON. LOVE & KISSES. XXX"

COLUMBUS? BALTIMORE? THOUGHT YOU WERE IN DETROIT? He texted her back.

LONG STORY. TELL YOU LATER. KISSES. KASEY.

The house began to fill with neighbors, former coworkers, teachers from the local university, and friends of Brad. He kept looking at his phone to check for messages. Hours later, it was halftime in the football game, and she was long overdue. The worry was evident on his face. Everyone who came in was greeted by Jane and Hal and handed a plate. They picked up utensils and helped themselves to the turkey, maple ham, mashed potatoes, gravy, stuffing, and everything else that was laid out in grand buffet style in the Silver's kitchen. Everyone ate… everyone except for Brad.

It was still snowing and no Kasey.

Near the end of the next football game, Sam Kennesaw pulled into the crammed driveway in his U.S. postal service jeep. Sam had worked at the Silver farm all through college and would help whenever they needed an additional set of hands. He was a tall, good-looking former basketball player and had to duck under the now-drooping sign that proclaimed: WELCOME HOME KASEY.

"Sammy what are you doing working today? You know there's no mail delivery on Thanksgiving."

"Well," he grinned, "I was called out to drop off a shipment at the airport and then found a special delivery package for Brad."

"For me?" Brad asked.

"Yes, for you," he said as he stepped aside revealing a small, snow-covered figure standing behind him.

Brad recognized the smile instantly. He was on his feet and bounded towards them, shouting "Kasey!"

She smiled as he hugged her, and he lifted her off the ground planting a kiss on his lips.

"Hi, everybody. I want you all to meet Kasey Morgan… my new fiancée," he exclaimed with a large grin on his face.

Jane Silver saw the look of love and caring in her son's eyes. She also saw the look of surprise on Kasey's face. Jane looked at Hal, and her eyes told him everything.

Recovering from her son's shock announcement, she went to Kasey and hugged her. "Welcome to Vermont and to our home. I'm Jane and this is Hal, Brad's dad." Hal hugged her and looked at his son.

"Sorry I'm late," she whispered, "but they kept cancelling my flights because of the storm. It is so good to meet you both at last. Brad has told me so much about the two of you."

"Better late than never," responded Jane with a smile.

Kasey shook the snow off her coat and smiled. "Do you normally get snowstorms so early here?" she asked. Her tender eyes and warm smile won Jane over in an instant.

"No never," said Hal with Jane and Brad saying at the same time, "Yes, all the time." The tension was broken, and they all laughed and made their way to the kitchen. They mingled with departing guests, and soon it was just the four of them.

Kasey helped Jane clear the tables, finish washing the dishes, and clean up after a wondrous meal. As the day ended, they finally all sat down together around the kitchen table.

They talked until the early morning getting to know her, and Jane could see the changed look on her young son's face, calm but excited. He was in love. Hal regaled Kasey with stories of Brad's youth, showing her pictures from a photo album of Brad's childhood. He told her how much he meant to them and the community. "He's a true Vermont mountain man."

Kasey drew in a deep breath and told them. "I'm sorry about the surprise announcement about our engagement just now. Brad promised me he would not say anything until I had a chance to talk with both of you first, but you know how he can be."

His mother grinned at her young son. "That's our Brad."

She smiled a terse, nervous smile before she continued. "The reason I asked him not to say anything is… we're not getting married."

"What?" Brad asked and stood looking at her.

She reached for his hand and gently guided him back to his seat.

"You must understand. I come from a very small close-knit family in Louisiana before moving to Florida. It was just me and my brother and my mom and dad. We were very close, like the three of you, but when my brother moved to Los Angeles to get married, my parents were devastated. I don't think they ever got over it. I went to college locally so I could be near them. It's a lesson I will never forget. I know that Brad loves me and he adores the two of you, but I was determined never to cause that kind of pain in anybody, else's life. I now see how much Brad loves the both of you. I can't take him away from all of this, and I can't live here with the work that I do."

"Why would you say something like this?" Brad asked.

"Because I love you, and I don't want you or your family to be miserable just because we want to get married and move to Florida. It's for the best. I now see I can't take you away from here. I'm sorry." She stood and hugged him, tears forming in her eyes. Jane could tell she was torn.

"I'm not letting you go," Brad pleaded. "I won't. I love you and I want to marry you," he said defiantly.

"Yes , I know you do, my sweet, but you will thank me for this in the years to come when you meet someone locally and decide to get married and have a family," she said with tears now streaming down her face.

"I don't understand." He paused and looked at her, "Is there someone else? Don't you love me?"

"Yes, I love you more than anything in the world, but I wanted to meet your family and see you here, in Vermont with all your friends. When I saw you here for the first time with everyone, I knew I could never take you away from all of this. I'm so sorry, Brad. The last thing in the world I ever wanted to do was to hurt you."

She stroked his face with her hand and with her voice cracking said, "It has been a long day, can you show me to my room?" It was very late, and tears clouded her eyes. "Good night Mr. and Mrs. Silver. I hope I didn't spoil your party. I have really enjoyed meeting you. My flight back to Florida leaves tomorrow night."

Shocked, they didn't know how to respond. "Good night, Kasey," Jane finally said. "We'll talk in the morning I'm sure. Good night…and it's Jane and Hal. Okay?"

"Thanks for everything… Jane."

Brad walked her upstairs, and his parents heard voices whispering above them from the second floor.

Hal and Jane went outside by the now-dying fire in the old stone fire pit. He cleared away the snow on the nearby bench. They sat and drank maple cocoa fortified with brandy. "First the news of Kasey," Jane said, "then the news of her visit and then Brad moving away, now the announcement of the wedding being called off… it's all too much to handle."

"Yes, but Janey did you see the way Brad looked at her?" whispered Hal.

"I did, but more importantly did you see the way she looked at him? It must be tearing them both apart inside."

She snuggled against her tall Vermont mountain man. The man she had loved for decades, the man made of granite now talking like a lovesick schoolchild and heartbroken father. The days and years of working on the farm had drained him; she could see it in his eyes. His pearl-grey eyes once so bright with enthusiasm for living now covered with layers of weariness. She clung to his arm and touched his face with her fingertips.

Hal looked at her. He was going to make it work; his family was counting on him. Hal pulled her close kissing her forehead. "It'll be fine, Janey. Don't worry. We'll make do somehow."

"I know it'll be fine. It always works out, and I have faith in you." She touched his square chin and kissed him. "I love you," she said pulling him close.

"I love you too."

The next morning over pancakes and some of the finest maple syrup in Vermont, it was just the family... and Kasey.

Hal poured coffee for everyone and stopped beside Kasey saying, "We're going to miss you Kasey, and even though we've only known you since yesterday, you won us over. We want you in the family—our family—and I won't take no for an answer."

"But Mr. Silver I told you last night that—"

He set the coffee pot back on the stove and pulled up a seat next to Jane. "I know what you said, but I've had the whole night to think about this. I..." he paused and looked at Jane, "we want the two of you to go to Florida if that is what you truly want... if that will make you happy."

"Yes but..."

"Let me finish, please." Hal gently touched her shoulder before proceeding, "The Silver family has run this farm for over eighty years, and it has been very good for us. We think it's time to let another family enjoy the fruits and pleasure of owning the best maple farm in the Northeast. I have had countless inquires about selling the farm over the years, and I know it won't be difficult to sell. The Maguire family approached me yesterday with an offer to buy the farm ... a very nice offer. It will take a couple of months to finalize, but I think we can manage until we do sell it." He paused and looked at the stunned faces of those he loved sitting around the table.

"Sell Silver Maple Farm?" Brad asked incredulously.

"Yes, it's the right time to sell the farm regardless of what happens with the two of you in Florida. It's way past time. I want to take my queen somewhere warm where she can wear sandals year round and drink pina coladas on the beach and maybe someday… watch our grandchildren grow up. That is if you don't mind having us around."

"Of course, but are you sure?" said Kasey, her eyes glistening with tears.

"Yes I'm… we're sure."

Jane put her arms around him and hugged him, tears flowing down her cheeks.

"Never more sure of anything in my life, but enough of this sappy, sticky sentimental stuff," Hal remarked in jest, with a newfound grin on his face that until now had been erased by years of sorrow. "Your flight doesn't leave until later on this afternoon, let's show Kasey what the best maple tree farm in Vermont really looks like and then when we come back we can sit down and have a grand lunch with some maple ham.

Now the whole family, including its newest member Kasey, was in tears and hugged one another

"Who's for some hot cocoa first, with the freshest maple sugar in all of Vermont?" asked ebullient Jane Silver. She was the happiest she had been in years and kissed her tall Vermont mountain man husband. Brad held out his hand to Kasey and they walked to the kitchen hand in hand. Life was good at the Silver Maple Farm once again.

# The Beautiful Redhead

Late at night, when I knew he was fast asleep, I again sneaked into my husband's den to read his private journal. I had learned a lot about him. I knew he was one of a kind, a good man, but I felt he was having an affair and in love with someone else. I had to know. I just had to find out. They say you should never read anyone's secret journals, but my curiosity pulled me in. I loved reading his daily notes but was shocked when I stumbled upon his most recent entry.

Journal Entry:

August 19—

She was an intoxicating redhead and I fell in love with her from the first moment I saw her. I had to have her. She cast a spell over me with her sexy "come hither" voice, and I must admit I was lost in my desire for her. I was passionately in love with her. She made me do crazy things, wild things that would have been beyond my comprehension before I met her. I knew I had to be careful when we met.

I loved being with her and taking her to secret places she had never been before. We went for wild rides on the beach and ran from the authorities when they discovered we were trespassing. I can still hear them shouting at us as we left them behind in a cloud of sandy ocean spray.

My blood surged and my pulse raced every time I was near her. I cast an admiring glance at her when we parted for the evening, savoring the soft curves of her beautiful figure. I was crazy in love and overlooked her minor faults and her growing temper tantrums. They became worse and worse. Did my wife suspect my feelings for her?

Soon, my lifelong friends began to talk in whispers that I should do something about her… but my GOD, how I loved her. They said she had extravagant tastes and would drain my bank account, but I didn't care. It was a love affair. I didn't know how it would end, but I knew it would end badly. I had to keep my love for her a secret.

She became more unpredictable in a predictable sort of world. We would be late many times due to her growing desire to do exactly what she wanted, regardless of the place or time. My feelings no longer seemed to matter to her.

When I was with her, I could not keep my hands off her, loving her even as I searched for a solution to the problem of how to part ways with my gorgeous redhead. I knew I could not live without her, and it was becoming more difficult to stay with her.

My hand was finally forced when she decided at the last moment she didn't want to go on our secret rendezvous weekend. She wouldn't budge, and I felt hopeless. I could not go by myself, it was the last straw.

The next morning with an aching desire in my heart and tears in my eyes, I left behind a goodbye note:

RED SPORTS CAR FOR SALE
TWO-SEATER FERRARI TESTAROSSA (REDHEAD)
LOVINGLY MAINTAINED
NOW AVAILABLE TO A GOOD HOME

I thought I heard a muffled cry as I walked away. I could not bear to turn around, afraid my resolve would weaken, but it was time to say goodbye…, goodbye to my beautiful redhead.

"Damn him," I whispered. My husband knew all along I had been reading his journal. I put it away, never to read it again and I learned my lesson. I also hid my own diary deep inside my chest of drawers. That was a close one.

# The Mountain

She saw the white-tipped mountaintop through the small window in her sparsely furnished room. It soared majestically above the countryside. Maybe today was the day she would reach the peak or... maybe tomorrow. It did not matter when, just that she made the valiant effort to conquer it and fill her time.

The mountain beckoned her with its compelling siren song pulling her closer to its bosom. Time to go she told herself, stretching her tired and aching limbs, wakening them from a fitful sleep on the hard bed inside the cold room.

She looked again outside and saw the green pathway starting point at the mountain's base, and soon she was there.

As usual, she went through her mental checklist to ensure she had everything she would need for her climb. She checked for extra socks, climbing boots, layer upon layer of clothes, ropes, ice hammers, mountain rations, and all of the other essentials critical for her climb.

When her list was complete, she registered at the base camp, as required of all climbers, to alert them of her intent to again climb the devil mountain by herself. Once more, she endured their daily taunts about traveling alone and the danger of the sometimes treacherous weather as one neared the peak. She had been here many times before over the past twelve months, but she felt that maybe today was the day she would make it to the top.

They bid her farewell as she made her way up the well-worn path to the summit. The countless minions who had gone before her had made the green grass threadbare. The early morning frost caused the grass to crunch under her boots as she began her march, her walking stick in hand.

After climbing for two hours, she checked her watch to time her ascent and saw she was ahead of her schedule. When she stopped later to rest, she could see the village far below her and knew her time was the best she had ever made. Invigorated, she pressed on.

The grassy path became more sparse the higher she climbed, now replaced by rocks, stones, and patches of snow. The air was thinner, and the temperature was dropping quickly.

The clouds in the sky ahead spelled trouble as she saw their message of snow and ice. The rocks, when coated with ice, were slippery, treacherous, and many times deadly. Her every step was now a strategic one as she continued her journey. For hours she climbed, the time weighing on her bones, the marrow chilled with every labored step she took.

The village below was now hidden by the clouds beneath her. She had to hurry or she would be defeated. She could not allow that to happen.

Higher and higher, she climbed. The air was thinner now and attacked her lungs with every breath she took. Ice began to form around her nose and mouth as she breathed. Her breathing became more difficult the higher she climbed.

She took a break to add another layer of clothing, but it was of little use, the cold found the cracks in her armor. Time to move on; she had lost time.

Hours passed and visibility grew worse and more dangerous. Icy wind bit her face, and it soon began to sleet and snow. She did not see the ice on the rock as she placed her foot down causing her to slip and slide backwards some twenty feet, losing her backpack down an icy ravine.

*Damn!*

Lying on her back, she saw the mountain peak not far from her. So near yet so far. It was lunacy to proceed without her supplies, but she had never made it this far before. The day was losing light as the cloud shrouded sun drifted behind the awesome peak.

She was doomed. She could make it to the top of the mountain, but it would be impossible to make it back down safely without her lost supplies.

*The hell with it!*

She lunged forward determined to complete her trek. The winds pushed her back, lashing her, ripping her face. The peak pulled her like some strange magnet, pulling her closer and closer. She was going to press on even though she may never come back alive. She stood tall and began again. Her hands were cold. Once more, she started up the mountain her head down to watch her footing and stop the biting wind from...

CLANG. CLANG. CLANG. The loud metallic sound broke her thoughts and shattered her silent world. The sound of squeaky metal hinges filled the air.

It was then she heard the familiar voice behind her say, "Prisoner number 2987, come forward. Dinner."

The jailer set the metal dinner tray on the wooden stool near the wall and left, closing the unjust cell door behind him without uttering another word. He was her only daily human contact. She trudged over to retrieve her tray and utensils and ate the same cold meal served day after day.

Turning, she looked through her small cell window at the disappearing mountaintop in the distance. She sat on the small stool and ate without looking at the food in front of her, with her eyes transfixed on the last rays of sun reflecting off the peak. "Tomorrow…, tomorrow, I will conquer you," she said. "But you will never conquer me."

# Mail-Order Bride

"Good mornin,' sodbuster."

"Mornin' Sam."

"You back here agin.'"

"Yup."

"How many days you been comin' and waitin' for her?"

"Seven days, countin' today."

"Think she'll be on the 10:20?"

"Don't know." The tall farmer dressed in worn jeans and grey suspenders looked to the sky. They had not had rain in weeks, and the parched crops were thirsty for relief.

"Another scorcher today, huh Jed? No rain for awhile ain't good fer crops, just loads of dust swirlin,'… dust to dust, so to speak. It just keeps blowin' right in your face. Stings somethin' fierce too."

"Yup."

"Looks like some clouds over there, sodbuster."

Jed looked up. "Nope… that's white smoke from the 10:20 Eastern. It's comin' down the tracks."

"Good luck, sodbuster. I got to let everyone know the train's a comin'."

"Thanks Sam."

The stationmaster's loud voice broke the morning silence. "Listen up, anyone waiting for the 10:20 train comin' in from the Saint Louis. The train's gonna stop here for fifteen minutes to take on water, and then I'll call for everybody to be onboard. Here she comes, watch the steam, you all. Fifteen minutes then all aboard."

The train pulled into the station in a puff of steam and the squeal of brakes. Only an old salesman in a coat and rumpled tie got off carrying his old leather sample bag slung over his shoulder. He tipped his hat to Sam, smiled, and proceeded on his way into the small dirt-filled town.

"Nobody gettin' off, sodbuster?"

"Nope, Sam. Doesn't look like she made it today."

"See ya tomorrow?"

"Yep."

"Hey Jed…Jed there's somebody getting off… back there on the rear platform. Is that her?"

"I dunno. I only have an old picture of her. Could be. Maybe." He walked towards the tall woman in a long cotton dress, wearing a yellow sunbonnet while dragging two large suitcases behind her.

"Jed? Jed Parker, is that you?" she asked him, dropping her heavy load.

"Yup. You Katherine?"

"Yes indeed I am. Katherine MacAfee. I am so sorry for the delay, but I missed my second train coming out of Saint Louis, and then the rails got flooded out further down the tracks and they had to be reset. I am so sorry to keep you waiting."

"No matter. Good you made it, I guess. Katherine, that's a long name."

"Call me Kate, if it pleases you."

"Long name and long hair and red hair at that. Hope it ain't a fiery red temperament too." He stood and looked at her eyeing her up and down. "No time to wash long hair out here and water is like gold hereabouts." He looked at her. "You look different than your picture and… with red hair and all."

"I'll cut my hair. It's too long now anyhow."

"Katherine, do you know cookin', sewin,' blacksmithin,' calfin,' or plantin'?"

"No. I studied music, art, and dance back east. But I'm a quick learner. Call me Kate."

"The winters here are cold as ice running through the cracks in the cabin, and the summer's heat is like brandin' irons, hot metal against the skin that never stops burning. The wind never stops cuttin,' while the sand and dust rip your face and eyes, hurtin' like a mule kick over and over again. One day is like the day before, and friends are like the lone cloud in the sky, miles away and rarely seen."

Her body shook. "I don't take much, Jed. I smile easy and 'm very forgivin.' It's just… I have nowhere else to go. Nowhere Jed. I got no one." Her head drooped.

"My given name is Jedidiah, Kate. I work hard because farmin' is long, hard work. Life here is a harsh but only as tough as we make it. But come springtime the valleys are coated with flowers the colors of rainbows as far as the eye can see, with summer and fall bringin' the sweetest fresh fruit that your mouth can imagine. And at crop time everyone comes together to help with the pickin,' and golly… the harvest parties are something to behold."

"Sounds nice, Jed," she said with a mellow smile.

"We'll do just fine, Kate; it just may take some time. Come, take my hand, and stop your tearin.' It's startin' to rain." He offered his outstretched hand to her. "Best get your bags in the buggy. We need to get home before the bridges wash out. We got lots of work left to do today. Hop up next to me. Come on, time to go home. You comin' Kate?"

"Well Jed, I…"

"All aboard!"

# Things My Mother Told Me

"You married a good man."

"I know, Mom. Mike is very good to me and the kids, it's just that…"

"No buts… he adores you and those kids. You must be strong, dear. I'm counting on you to hold the family together."

"I will, Mom."

The sound of a car crash down the road caused them both to turn around to see if they could see anything. Nothing. The accident was too far away.

It was fall, and the weather was getting cooler. Way too early for snow even in Boston, but she thought she felt something wet brush against her cheek. Then she felt it again.

"I have so much to tell you and so little time," her mother said wringing her hands like she used to do when she was nervous. "Save your money; you're going to need it in your old age."

"Mom, we'll be fine. Mike has a good job, and with me selling real estate on the side… we'll be fine. Don't worry about us."

She fretted, showing her disapproval as mothers always do.

The sound of an ambulance came rushing by… then a second one.

"Bad accident," she whispered and grabbed her daughter's arm. "Hope no one's hurt real bad," she whispered.

She began to rush to tell her daughter what was on her mind. "Don't be too strict with the girls, not like I was with you. Keep the boys close and watch over them. Don't forget to poke the bottom of the pie pan with a fork before you add your filling. Dump your coffee grounds around your roses… it'll help 'em grow. Use a half of teaspoon of nutmeg when you make pasta and don't roll it too thin. Use all your coupons, save your money. Buy your Christmas cards and wrapping paper right after the holidays. Make time for just you and Mike. Walk the beach at sunrise and sunset. Hold his hand, tight. Kiss him a lot. Don't be afraid to touch him and tell him you love him. Don't forget to…"

She grabbed her mother's arm. "Mom, I love you, we'll be just fine. What are you so worried about?"

"I love you too, dear, it's just I have so much to tell you," she said as they walked arm and arm. "I don't even know where to begin."

They stopped walking and sat down on a park bench.

"I love it here. It's such a beautiful park. So restful." She reached out, picked a small yellow blossom from a nearby bush, and handed it to her daughter. "This is for you dear... to remember me by," she paused before continuing, "I still have so much to tell you, but you have to leave now," she said clutching her daughter's arm. "I don't know if I will ever see you..."

"Mrs. Johnson can you hear me? Mrs. Johnson? Your husband is on his way. You're in the emergency room at Saint Elizabeth's. Can you hear..."

She opened her eyes to chaos.

"Oh thank, God, we thought we lost you," said the young doctor peering into her eyes with a small flashlight.

A nurse inserted an IV in her arm and she felt her dab the blood away from her face. She saw the two of them turn and strained to hear them whisper to one another. "What about the mother?"

"She didn't make it. She died on impact. Damn drunk driver," he cursed through his clenched teeth.

Orderlies rushed by with gurneys. The sound of sirens filled the air as tears swelled in her eyes. The pain went straight to her heart as she mourned her loss. She went to wipe the tears from her eyes and noticed inside her hand her mother's gift... a small crumpled yellow flower.

*I love you, Mom.*

# The Painter from Syros

They walked together like identical twins for they had been married as long as the old fisherman had been fishing in these Grecian blue waters. When she walked to the market with him, she swayed to the right in her long black dress, black shoes, and matching shawl, and he leaned with her, his ailing hip betraying his age. His knee sometimes gave way after walking short distances, causing them to stop on occasion; just to rest, he would say.

Afterwards, they walked home from the bustling market near the harbor, back to their small cottage that overlooked the harbor town on the Greek Island of Syros. Years earlier his aching hip required him to stop fishing on the big fishing boats. He now dedicated himself, as always, to helping and being with her.

Each day remained the same as the day before. They rose to greet the sun and sat on their whitewashed porch watching the glistening windmills and the yellow morning orb rising over the blue-green waters below.

She boiled water to make churned coffee, grinding sugar with drops of cream, creating a fluffy moist latte for him, just the way he liked it. They ate their fruit and shared a small baguette from the village bakery acquired during their trip to the market the day before.

"*Kalimera, agapi mou,*" he greeted her.

"*Kaimera,* Stavros," she responded with a smile. "Another beautiful day... yes?

"Yes."

After washing up in the small basin and ensuring everything was in its proper place, she fetched her worn reed basket. They walked down the windy path towards the morning market for their daily shopping. The pair always stopped at the beautiful flowers they passed on their journey and breathed in the aromas from the waking blossoms.

"*Latrevo afta ta louloudia,*" he whispered.

"I love the flowers too," she responded. Her command of English was better than his because of the time she worked in her sister's tourist shop in town.

They gazed at each other and smiled the smile of years, that soft smile which said it all. She often held his arm, she said to stabilize herself, but he knew her footing was as stable as a mountain goat. She liked to be close to him as they walked together down the path.

The Greek countryside in this tiny village was shepherded by the white convent with its towering cross and blue doors perched high on top of the hill. The nuns prayed daily and sang their beautiful hymns that rang through the hillsides below. The nuns could be seen in the afternoon in small groups of two or three as they hurried through the small fishing village.

The old couple went to market every day to shop and to gossip with friends. Stavros left her there and returned to fish on the shore of the waters of his youth. He would fish for their supper, but now he fished from the shore with the young boys and other old men, the ones too old or too tired to fish from the big fishing boats.

Fishing on this warm day in July, he fought long for the reward of a red mullet trying to swim for freedom. Freedom or dinner were its choices, and at last, it had none; it was to be the banquet of the old fisherman and his bride.

When he saw her later, his dusty blue-grey eyes twinkled with recognition; he raised his prize for her to see and to share in his glory. Her hands clasped together, she smiled, and then gently stroked his hair, now white with age, but he was still her fisherman; he was the mighty Stavros.

Walking back through the village, past the small tourist stores selling nonsense items and porcelain windmills, he noticed the new English nun with her class of young children painting pictures of the boats lying at anchor in the harbor. He walked towards the small group and admired their work, but the paints seemed to only lay on the stretched canvas and were not as vibrant as one would hope.

The art teacher, a tall nun dressed in her blue and white linen habit, came forward towards him, "Good day, sir. Are you a painter?"

"No," his wife responded quickly. "He is a fisherman. He is Stavros, the best fisherman in the Southern Aegean." Obvious pride showed on her aged face.

"Nice picture," the old man said softly as he walked past them. "Pity they no capture colors so well. The colors of world change with light," he continued with the heavy accent of a second language.

"Show me what you mean," asked the inquisitive nun.

"No, no, I fisherman, no painter."

"But surely you can be both. Show me what you mean, please" pleaded the young, inexperienced nun. She held out a paintbrush and a fresh palette filled with colors. She motioned him to an empty chair with an easel and a canvas positioned in front.

He smiled as he took the brush and began to paint. He wielded it like a delicate instrument, with artistry and craft. He stroked the broad artist's knife, laying paint on the canvas in deep, dark colors, swirling left, then right, blues, reds, yellows appeared on the canvas, magically blending together. He added more color and worked with passion until he was finished. "Like that!" he proclaimed stepping away, refreshed.

The colors were so vivid, the drawing so insightful, passersby stopped to stare at the old man's handiwork. Having worked on it no longer than the time a butterfly spends on a flower; he had created something beautiful, something wonderful and magical. The young nun, amazed, was lost in a desert without words while she traveled his painting with her eyes, her soul stirred, her heart wept.

*"Ti kaneis edo? Ast'aftes tis vlakies! Idies!"* His wife commanded.

She tugged at his sleeve and repeated herself for the benefit of the young nun this time in English, "Enough of this foolishness. Stavros, it's time to go home." The glimmer that had lit his eyes suddenly dimmed as he returned the brush to its resting place on the easel.

"Thank you," is all he said, and they walked away in silence towards their cottage.

Storm clouds were brewing to the North over the hills and the wind turned brisk to chill the air spinning the hilltop windmills into a frenzy. He started the blackened fireplace to warm their small stone home and the hearts within the four walls.

She did her knitting, preparing for winter, while he sat dutifully across from her holding her yarn. She talked about the news gathered from town. Stavros looked down at his hand while he unwound another layer of yarn and noticed a small bit of blue and yellow paint on his long bony finger. His mind wandered, now filled with other paintings he dreamed of creating.

It rained the next day and the following day and the sun did not shine in their southern paradise. Days later, when the skies finally cleared, they yearned to take flight from the cottage and left early for town. The pair passed the nun in her blue artist garb working with her students and she waved hello.

"Good morning," she said with a young smile and hurried towards them. "I sold your painting to some Americans from the cruise ship that docked here this week. They loved your work." She held out her hand to offer him the coins that filled her palm.

His wife took them and shoved them into the hidden folds of her black dress, "*Hazo Amerikanakia!*" she whispered out loud to him. "Hah! No work at all. Everyone knows that ignorant American tourists will buy anything."

Not put off, the young nun responded, "Stavros, I can work with you and help you refine your work," explained the art teacher.

The wife stopped and looked hard at the youthful and inexperienced nun, obviously new to the island. She should have known not to call a stranger, and a married one at that, by his first name.

"My Stavros is not interested in your painting or your help." She turned to stare at him. "Come Stavros we have much work to do." He hobbled behind her walking towards town, turning once to glance in the direction of the young teacher, as he made his way to the fishing pier.

Later, at home, he filleted the fish he caught that day and prepared it for dinner. Afterwards he finished his small glass of ouzo before the small cozy fire while she knitted and he patiently held the yarn in his firm fisherman hands. He smiled with love as he good-naturedly held the bright woolen colors that she had chosen to use.

A few days later, she said she was going to visit her sister on the other side of the island. She had not seen her bedridden sibling for weeks and her sister begged her for companionship.

Stavros fished from the long wooden pier at the harbor with some friends and his catch was quite impressive. Later, as Stavros walked home, he saw the nun and her painting classes. The old man edged closer to the group pretending to look for a certain boat in the waters beyond.

The young nun saw him and smiled. She pulled a chair away from an empty easel and motioned for him to sit. He laid his catch on the grass under a nearby shade tree. The fish were restrained in a wet burlap sack as he took the brushes and palettes she offered.

The patient teacher gently guided his hands and showed him the wonders of light and the treacheries of darks. She held the brush stiff for the lines and soft for curves, then backed away from instructing him and watched him begin his work.

Slow at first, as if stepping into an unknown pool of water, he painted like other students until he found his sea legs, then the slashes of brilliant colors and shapes suddenly became alive on his canvas. The sun contained amber glory and the sea was foaming and wild as he continued to deliver stroke after stroke of paint, all in vibrant color. He used his old gnarled fingers to add paint from one side to the other imparting a bit of his soul with every stroke. He worked with passion without regard to time or place.

She noticed, walking behind him, that his work looked different depending on the view of the canvas. The paint was thick, curled, and deep and the colors seen on one side were hardly noticeable from the opposite side. The reds vibrant in one view were dull from the other and blues deep and shiny from the left, were calming and reflective from the right.

His painting said it in a convincing and contradicting fashion, the sea was calm, the sea was churning, the sun shone bright, the sun was violent. It was spellbinding to watch him create. He worked trancelike, with the fever of one possessed. It was not a race but a test of endurance to see who would win… the old fisherman, the paint, the colors, or the sea.

Finally, he was done and he sat before the young nun with her dull black shoes peeking out from beneath her uniform. She was breathless as she held her hands clasped before her, "Stavros, it is magnificent! And you have never painted before? You have had no training?" she asked.

He shook his head in response.

The grey-haired old man felt ten years younger, he felt alive in releasing the inner sprits from inside himself to their mighty perch on the canvas. He stood to begin his journey up the steep hill but turned, querying the young nun, "*Tha ithela na matho zografia!*"

She looked at him not understanding his dialect.

He repeated himself this time in broken English, "I lern to paint rooses. You teech? Me paint beetiful rooses?"

"Of course, Stavros, I am honored to help you learn to paint whatever you like," she said and noticed he appeared taller and somewhat younger, as he retreated up the hill towards his small white cottage.

Over the weeks that followed, the old couple resumed their daily walks to town, and she went to the market as he fished. Afterwards, instead of resting at the Taverna in the shade of the old lemon trees seeking relief from the scorching sun, he went to paint, forsaking his friends. Later he would meet his wife at their usual place.

Stavros came to paint every day for an hour or so. Finally, the nun could teach him no more because he had surpassed her own ability. His art was like that of the masters, firm yet soft, simple but elegant, turbulent but calm. The nun was amazed at his handiwork.

It was heavenly, and all he wanted to do was to paint. He loved to paint more than anything else he had ever done. He painted memories of his youth, fishing with his father, cooking with his mother, wrestling with his brothers and all of the sunsets he remembered. Then he thought of his wife, the twinkle of her smile, the flowers they picked, the days they fought and the nights they made up.

His wife finished at the market early one day and saw a crowd milling around the art class with everyone watching someone paint. She parted the crowd and found her Stavros sitting there painting.

The crowd was mesmerized by his artwork, his depth of color and vision. He was reaching their souls through his painting.

She had found his secret passion, and she called to him, angry, "Stavros! It is time to go home," she commanded.

He laid down the brush and stood immediately and obediently trudged behind her up the hill. He loved her so.

It was quiet for a while until she said, "I don't like it that you paint. You don't have time for such foolishness. Do you hear me? What will people say? Stavros the painter? Ha!" They walked the rest of the way in silence.

He turned around one last time to view his handiwork.

Over the next few days, she found busy work for him around the cottage. "You like to paint so much? The doors and shutters need a new coat of blue paint and the cottage has not been painted in two years. Now do something useful." He spent the days painting the walls, the doors, the shutters and the rest of the cottage. At night he held her knitting yarn in silence, while she talked about her days spent in the village, laughing. He did not mind, he loved her so.

Some days later she told him she had an appetite for fish, fresh fish not salted ones and that he should go into town and catch some fish.

He put on his old wool jacket, for there was a chill in the air, donned his cap and lit his pipe as he walked alone down the familiar path, past the students with their easels. The young nun waved and motioned for him to join in the class. His head shook side to side in silence as he strode past her without looking further. The clouds were brewing from the North and he predicted a storm with strong wind and rain. His years as a fisherman had taught him many things.

The pier was filled with other old fishermen, and he was forced away from the crowds, to the rocks, past the old abandoned fishing pier to the deeper water. He flung his line out to the darkest water where the bigger fish often were. The sky was shadowed by the now forming clouds, the wind slapped his face, and he knew it was not good fishing weather. But she wanted fresh fish and he was going to catch the biggest fish for her. He was Stavros the Fisherman.

He cast his lure far, but his line came back empty. He flung it out again, further this time than he had before and soon he felt an urgent tug and then a strong pull from the line. It raised high above the water before it went deep, out of sight.

The fish was strong and tried to run, pulling against the old man's chest. He held it with all his might then he lowered the rod, turning the reel slowly before arching it high above his head. His arms were like iron but this fish had a will to survive. The old man had been in many fights like this before, but this fish was like no other.

It took all of the old man's strength to pull the fish close. He walked deeper into the water towards his foe, the fish pulling, twisting, turning, trying to endure and get away… to escape his fate. He reeled the fish in and soon it tired from the fight and began to face the inevitable.

He pulled hard and saw it was a large black grouper, the largest he had ever caught. Holding the line tight, he moved back towards the shore. It was then he saw it, lurking below the surface, the deadly scorpion fish. Before he could move, the venomous stinger punctured his ankle and he could feel the hot poison surge through his foot. He fled, giving his prize catch his freedom to live another day.

Stavros felt the warmth of the venom and the cold from lack of circulation traveling up his leg. He made his way to the doctor's office off the main square.

The wound was fresh but potent the doctor told him, surveying the puncture. He cleansed it, and gave Stavros some medicine for later. "Do you believe in prayer?" he asked Stavros. He told him to remain quiet for the next couple of days and time would tell if he had been stung by a pesky youngster or an angry deadly adult. Stavros made his way home and was greeted by his wife.

"Where is my fresh fish?" she demanded until she saw his bandaged foot.

The poison had traveled from his ankle to his knee and he nearly collapsed from the pain. She put him to bed. His fever began to boil, and he was delirious thinking of sunsets, fishing, and painting. He thought of his mother and his family, and as always, he thought of his wife.

His fever seemed to break some days later but his foot and leg turned green. His sight was failing as he lifted himself from the bed to the chair outside, to sit in the sun. If only he could paint one more time, that's all he wanted, just to paint one last time. Painting helped lift his mortal soul, but with his eyesight failing he was resigned to the fact he may never paint again.

Some days later, the young nun stopped by and left some paints and brushes for Stavros.

"I heard in town he was stung by a scorpion fish," she told his wife. "When he wakes tell him everyone has been asking about him and wanting to see more of his beautiful paintings. May these paints and brushes bring him cheer."

The wife looked at the paint things from the busybody nun and hid them in the small closet in the front room. "Foolishness," she muttered.

A few days later, the wife received word that her sister had taken a turn for the worse and had asked her to make one final visit. The old wife prepared a meal for Stavros and with peck on his cheek and promises of an early return, she was on her way. She said he looked much better.

In town, everyone made inquiries as to the health of her husband. How was he surviving after his treacherous encounter with the deadly scorpion fish? Was he still painting?

She was pleased that neighbors asked about her husband, even though she was angry they thought of him as a painter. He was Stavros the fisherman.

It was late that day, nearly evening, when she made her way home to the hillside cottage overlooking the Aegean Sea. She had stayed longer than she had expected, for her sister seemed to be feeling stronger the longer she stayed. As she approached the small gate in front of the cottage she was greeted by the young nun who inquired about her husband. Her first thought was to swat her away like a pesky fly, but she softened instead and invited her in for a visit.

As they approached the cottage she was alarmed to see the front door open, swaying mildly in a gentle breeze. She saw her husband sitting inside, in his large chair, sleeping.

The old wife waved a cheerful hello saying to him, "Stavros, I'm home." She received no response from him. As she and the nun entered the cottage, she bent over to kiss him only to find his forehead colder than the deepest water in the harbor.

She said his name once more, "Stavros!" Then again, "Stavros!" she said her voice rising with fear. Nothing! It was then the full impact hit her..., her Stavros was gone. He was dead. He had waited for her as long as he could but his time ran out. She knelt before him, grieving her largest tears and could not stop muttering his name, "Stavros, Stavros," she cried again and again falling to the floor near his feet.

The nun stood by her, unsure of how to comfort her. She noticed the door to the closet slightly ajar with something on the wall which she could not clearly see. She crept towards the door and saw the old man's painting palette and the colorful paints oozing onto the dark stone floor beneath it.

Pulling the wooden door handle, she opened it and the setting sunlight shone on the once unpainted rear wall, revealing the picture of the most beautiful woman she had ever seen. Tall and proud with rose-colored cheeks, wearing a white dress, a come-hither smile, and blue flowers in her hair. There was one word painted by her side, which said simply, *"Rose."*

She stepped back in awe of this *Mona Lisa*, captivating her like no other painting ever had before and whispered the name aloud, "Rose."

The old wife now stood from her dead husband's side to join the now sobbing nun and when she saw the painting of herself in her wedding dress, the river of tears began again.

Stavros had only wanted to learn one thing, how to paint the picture of his most beautiful Rose.

# Yes, Officer

"All right son, you know the drill. Spread 'em wide, hands on the cruiser."

"Yes, Officer."

"Anything in your pockets I need to know about?"

"No, Officer."

"What's this, a stuffed animal?"

"It's called a Crazy Pug Bear, a gift for my daughter, Officer."

"Is this what you stole from the toy store? Is this what they called the police about?"

"Yes, sir."

"You in the military son, what's with the haircut, tattoo, and all?"

"Yes, sir, the Marine Corps."

"*Semper Fi*, and all that, huh?"

"Yes, Officer."

"Are you stupid or something, son? You stealing this stuffed bear from the store is going to land you in jail. Damn, I've heard it all, now. Put your hands behind your back, and don't you dare try anything, you hear?"

"Yes, sir."

"You have the right to remain silent. Anything you say can and will be used against you in a court of law. You have the right to speak to an attorney. If you cannot afford an attorney, one will be appointed for you. Do you understand these rights as they have been read to you?"

"Yes, Officer."

"Damn, can't you say anything other than, 'Yes Officer'?"

"Officer, you dropped something out of my wallet, there, there on the ground."

"This picture? Who is this pretty little thing?"

"That's my pride and joy officer, that's my Mattie, my little girl."

"Mattie? What kind of name is that?"

"It's short for Madeline, Officer. She was named after her grandmother."

"I'll hold onto your wallet until we get to the station. Watch your head son. Slide into the back of the cruiser."

"Yes, sir."

"Just settle in, we'll be back to the station in no time."

"Are you married, Officer?"

"No."

"Ever been in the service, Officer?"

"Yeah, sure was son, Navy. Saw lots of tattoos like yours. First I was assigned to Military Police, then to the submarine *USS Cheyenne*, then back to MP duty in Subic Bay the Philippines."

"Boomer, huh?"

"Yeah, sailed the seven seas on a tiny, cramped, rollin' tincan, but loved every minute of it and I really loved the Philippines."

"How long were you in for, Officer?"

"Eighteen years."

"God, you were almost a lifer. You had only two more years to go before retirement. Why did you get out so early?"

"Well…I stopped getting letters from my wife, and she wouldn't answer my overseas phone calls. I had friends go by our house, and they said it was vacant. She skipped town with my kid."

"Damn, that hurts."

"Yeah, I tried getting Compassionate Leave to go home and find out what was going on, but no go. I jumped ship in Norfolk then spent two years hunting for her and her new boyfriend. Found them in Albuquerque, New Mexico. She was working as a waitress, and he was a mechanic. They were two of the sorriest losers you ever wanted to meet, but that kid of mine, she's like gold."

"What happened, Officer?"

"I went to take my little girl back home, and they called the cops. Her mechanic buddy tried to stop me, and I broke his jaw. I got arrested for assault. They let me go when they found out that they both had multiple outstanding arrest warrants pending against them from three states for burglary and grand theft."

"What happened with the Navy?"

"My commanding officer went to bat for me and got me a discharge rather than being charged as a deserter. He helped me land this job here in my hometown with the Dallas Police Department. He saved my life and that of my little girl."

"Is that your little girl's picture on the dashboard, Officer?"

"Yeah, that's her, fifteen now, she's a heartbreaker. It bugs her because I want to meet all of her dates before they take her out. The boys freak out when they see the police car in the driveway. But deep down inside she loves it that I care so much."

"Yes, officer. I remember this neighborhood growin' up as a kid here. That was before it was taken over by all of the gangs and before I went into the Marine Corps. Neighborhood sure has changed. My house is just down this road."

"You grew up here?"

"Yes, sir, before I went into the Marine Corps."

"Why did you come back?"

"My wife died six months ago of an overdose. I got Compassionate Leave from the Marines to come home for my daughter's birthday. I used all the money that I had in the bank to get back here. I wanted to get her a birthday present, but I ran out of money. I don't know how I'll pay for the ticket back to California when I get out of jail and report back for duty."

"What about your little girl?"

"My sister is going to take care of her for the next six months until I get out of the Marine Corps. I already have a job lined up at Akers Hardware as an assistant manager or at least I did have a job lined up."

"What do you mean?"

"They don't hire anyone with a criminal record."

"You know I have to take you in son, don't you?"

"Yes, officer, I understand. You're just doing your duty. Just like we all have to…we all have to do our duty."

"Is that why you stole that teddy bear, for your daughter's birthday?"

"Yes, Officer. I have disappointed her so many times before I didn't want to disappoint her again, ever."

"How much was that bear, son?"

"It was thirty-nine dollars, Officer."

"You risked your freedom for thirty-nine dollars?"

"Yes, sir, but I've risked my life for a hell of a lot less, sir."

"I understand but wait just a moment. Hold on son, I am pulling the car over. That bear cost less than fifty-dollars and therefore it's up to the discretion of the responding officer. I am going to see that the store gets the money back for the bear and you get home to your little girl, do you hear me?"

"But Officer, I don't have the money to pay for the bear."

"I know that, dimwit. You already paid for it overseas and don't even realize it. Here, take the bear, and I had better not ever catch you stealing around here again, you understand me? I'll square it with the store. Now git. Here's your wallet back with the picture of your little girl."

"Officer, this wallet has three-hundred dollars in it."

"Are you saying there was more money in before?"

"No sir, my wallet was empty when I gave it to you officer. I had no…"

"I told you git, now. I mean it, before I change my mind."

"Yes, Officer. Thank you."

"No, thank you, son. Say Happy Birthday to your little girl for me."

"Yes, Officer, and give your little girl a hug from a fellow GI. Thank you."

"I plan to do that right now, son. Good night."

# Jig

The hotel lobby was full and very busy. Bellmen in their green and gold velvet jackets hustled push carts loaded with luggage across the white marble floor as they ushered in the newest guests. The Grand Hotel lived up to its name, big, cold, and quite grand with its shiny loud floors sounding the comings and goings of its guests. Tall windows in the lobby let in the bright streaming sunshine. A young girl, barely ten, ran through the lobby, her long red hair flying about her.

A tall elegantly dressed woman beckoned her, "Ravenna, stop running. Come here."

"Mummy, will we be here much longer? If we are I'll need to use the loo."

"I'll take you to the bathroom in just a little while my dear," the mother responded, tacking the one untamable wild red hair behind the child's ear and straightening the Spanish gold cross, which hung crooked about her neck.

"But Mummy we've been here forever. I want to go back to Dublin. When does our boat leave? Will father be there to greet us when we arrive? Do we have time for more shopping before we leave? Mummy, I'm so hungry."

"Quiet child, there will be plenty of time for everything we want to do. Just sit. We will have lunch a little later."

"But I'm so hungry now."

"You just finished breakfast, my sweet."

"Yes, I know, but I want one last American hamburger before we leave, just one more, please, please Mummy?"

"Maybe later, Ravenna, now come here and sit down. He should be here soon."

Crowds thinned as the lull between check-in and checkout at the hotel took place. Men in dark suits with newspapers rushed for lunchtime appointments. She saw trucks going by outside as the sun disappeared and it started to rain. Plump umbrellas appeared on the street outside, hiding busy New Yorkers, who once again were rushing everywhere.

"Who are we waiting for Mummy?"

"An old friend of mine from years ago dear, an American."

"Does Father know this American friend?"

"No dear, it was before your father's time."

"Mummy, I must go to the loo. I see it there in the lobby. Is it okay, Mummy? I'll come right back."

"All right, dear, but don't get lost, once we meet with my friend we'll be leaving. Now don't dally anywhere Ravenna. You come right back. Do you hear me?"

"Yes, Mummy." She was off, skipping her way across the lobby.

Men with exceedingly beautiful women on their arms hustled past the front desk. The elevator bell sounded, and they went straight to the top. No one seemed to take notice.

She saw him enter the lobby, tall but more distinguished looking. His hair, now thinner and gray with only wisps of red intermingled. He had added more weight since she had seen him last, heft that comes with success, at least twenty pounds, two pounds for every year she guessed. The added girth made his dark suit fit tight around his stomach. She laughed inside at the irony. His expensive silk tie peeked from underneath his buttoned jacket. He unbuttoned his jacket to let some air out. She laughed again.

Their eyes met; a wistful smile crept to his lips.

The strong smell of spiced after-shave lingered after he kissed her on the cheek.

"Hello Jig…how are you?" he asked.

"Fine Governor, just fine, but I told you I would be fine and I am just that, fine." She felt ill at ease and immediately regretted her decision to call him.

"Still the same old Jig, huh?"

"Some things never change."

"Yes that's true. You know… I waited for you at the doctor's office in Madrid, but you never showed."

"Yes, I never showed. But things are fine now, Governor. Just fine."

"I've missed you, Jig. I was glad when you called yesterday. It's so good to see you. Do you have time for a drink? For old times' sake?"

"No, I must be going soon. I just didn't feel right being in New York and not calling, at least to say hello."

"I'm glad you called. I was not sure what to think, what to make of our meeting place."

"Think nothing of it. It was just a convenient place for me, that's all."

"Are you happy, Jig? Truly happy?"

"Yes, I am. I moved back to Dublin and married a barrister. We live in the country, and we have a wonderful life together and ahh… here comes the treasure in my life that makes me the most happy. She's just barely ten but going on twenty," she said with a weak smile.

"Ravenna come here and meet an old friend of Mummy's." She looked in his direction. An awkward silence surrounded them as their eyes met. "This is my daughter, Ravenna. "

The young girl held out her hand, "Good day, sir, it is a pleasure to meet you." She smiled at him.

"She loves to sing the Irish Ballads and dance the Irish Jig I taught her."

"Mummy, can we go now? I'm famished."

"Come darling, we are leaving now. Goodbye, Governor. See I told you it would fine, just fine."

# What a Woman Says

(Words that women use and men need to know—now)

"I think it's time for me to have a conversation with Alex. He's old enough, and with him getting married soon I need to speak to him about some things," he said as his loving wife was clearing the table and began washing the dishes from dinner.

"You can do it now if you like while I do the dishes."

He looked at her in awe. She balanced a professional job, all the kids' sports programs, ran the household, shopped, cooked the dinners, and made sure the kids got to school on time. She was incredible. Even after twenty-five years of marriage, he could not walk past her without touching her, slightly caressing her bottom, or kissing her neck.

He went to the fridge and poured her a glass of white wine. "Tell you what," he told her. "You go upstairs, draw a warm bath, put on some soft music, and have a glass of wine while I clean up here and have a chat with Alex."

"I love you," she said kissing him on the cheek while laying a wet handprint on his right buttock. "Don't be too long," she said with a twinkle in her eye before she walked up the steps, wine glass in hand, humming an unknown tune. He watched her disappear, her swaying behind enticing and beckoning him.

"Alex! Come in here and help me with the dishes," he said as he began to wash the plates from supper. He waved at him in the other room.

His sullen twenty three year old son appeared at the doorway, his music ear-buds drowning out anything his father had to say.

"Turn it off," his father motioned to him. "We need to have a talk."

"About what?" he asked while unplugging himself from his wired world and already missing it.

"We need to talk about women. It's important."

"I had that talk in the sixth grade dad. Been there, done that," he replied as he reinserted his ear buds to listen to his music. He stood and watched his father.

"Not this one," his dad said, gently extracting the device from his ears. "This is about what women say and what they mean. They are two different things entirely but if you prefer to listen to your music instead be my guest. You can go into your marriage with Heather next year and learn for yourself... the hard way," he said as he finished washing the dishes. "However, it's only the most important piece of information you'll ever hear."

The dishes done and put away he poured himself a glass of wine and surveyed the kitchen before retreating to the TV room. He left the kitchen perfect... tidy, clean and everything in its place.

"What do you mean Dad? Tell me."

He now had his son's full attention. "Sit, listen, and learn. Are you ready?"

"Yeah, yeah!"

"There will be many times in your life that you will argue with Heather," he began solemnly. "Always be the first to apologize even if you're right and you think it's her fault. Even if you have no idea what the argument is about... apologize. Especially if she is pregnant. Just go ahead and apologize. And do it quickly... but be sincere."

"Apologize? What if I'm not wrong?"

"Like I said, apologize anyway. There will be many times over the course of your marriage that you'll be wrong and you won't be caught." He stopped and looked at his son. *He has a lot to learn about women.*

"Now, when you do fight, and you will, many times, believe me, you will come to a standstill and your wife will utter one fateful word, and that word is... *fine*. Be careful son... there's danger! *Fine*...this is the word women use to end an argument when they are right, and you need to shut up. Just shut up and learn. Okay?"

"Got it," said the young protégé.

"Next, there'll be times when you'll be rushing to a movie or a ballgame or a party or a wedding or something and you'll ask your darling bride if she is ready and she'll say... give me *five minutes*. If she is getting dressed, this means a half an hour or longer. Just be prepared to wait as long as it takes."

"How long? She said it would only be five minutes."

"Five minutes is only five minutes if she gave you five more minutes to watch the game before helping out around the house. Just be patient, and whatever you do don't look at your watch. Just pull out your phone and play some games or something and ... be prepared to wait for an hour or so. Got it?"

"Yeah, I got it!"

"Now if you're having an argument and she says the magical word *nothing*—then this is the calm before the storm. This means something, and you should be on your toes. Arguments that begin with *nothing* usually end in *fine*. Got it?"

"Okay, got it."

"Now sometimes you may want to do something or go somewhere with the guys and you want to ask her or tell her what is going on. Be careful when she says *go ahead*. This is a dare, not permission. Don't Do It! All right?"

"All right, Dad," he said as he began to write everything down as if it were the Holy Scriptures.

"Now we get to the important stuff. Listen close. Be alert to what I call... *the loud sigh*. This is not actually a word, but is a nonverbal lethal statement often misunderstood by men. A loud sigh means she thinks you are an idiot and wonders why she is wasting her time standing there and arguing with you about nothing. Remember the word we talked about earlier—the word *nothing*? Be very careful!"

"Got it, Pop."

"Now to the dangerous stuff. When she utters the phrase *that's okay*. Well... this is one of the most dangerous statements a woman can say to a man. *That's okay* means she wants to think long and hard before deciding how you will pay for your mistake. Got it? It may take a very long time just don't forget that she warned you. Got it?"

"Yeah."

A little while later a voice from the upstairs bedroom rang out, "Honey, are you coming to bed?"

"Soon, baby." He turned back to his son.

"Got it," he said writing furiously on his long yellow notepad.

"Now be really careful when the woman you love says *whatever*, it's woman's way of saying SCREW YOU! Okay?

"Now when she says *thanks*—be careful. When a woman says thanks... you do not question or faint. Just say 'you're welcome.' Unless she says *Thanks a lot*—that is PURE sarcasm and something very different. She is not thanking you at all. DO NOT under any circumstances say 'you're welcome.' That will bring on a '*whatever*.'"

"God, Pop, that's a lot to remember. How do you keep it all straight?"

"Practice, practice, and practice."

"Now the most critical piece, when a woman says, '*Don't worry about it, I got it.*' This is another dangerous statement, meaning this is something that a woman has told you to do several times, but she is now doing it herself. This will later result in a man asking "What's wrong?" The woman will say *whatever*—and we both know where that leads. So be careful!

"Jerry, are you coming up?" his wife queried him again from upstairs, only louder.

He turned to his son and whispered, "One last thing, when the woman in your life calls you and asks you if you are coming to bed there is only one answer—*yes, dear.*"

"Yeah, Dad, but God that's a lot to remember even with all my notes." He had a puzzled look on his face as he read his notes. "I'm gonna read through my notes and stay up and play some video games. All right, Dad?"

"Well, you have to be at work early tomorrow, but it is up to you if…"

"Now?" came the insistent remark from upstairs.

"And when she says the word—*now*—it means now, not in ten seconds or ten minutes—*now*. This is only lesson number one with more to follow, okay, got it? … Yes, dear. Coming. Good night, Alex."

"Good night, Dad."

The young son played some games for a while before he picked up his phone and called his fiancé. "Hey baby, what's goin' on?"

"Not much, just sitting here thinking of you. Are you coming over tomorrow night?"

"I was meaning to tell you, I was thinking about going out with the guys and watchin' the game. Is that okay?"

"Yeah, sure… *fine, whatever.*"

# Mighty Miss

"Oh Jake, will you look at this place? Our home! You can see where the river came right through our living room then out the kitchen door. Look how high the water came up. Lookie here, Jake, it's like a dirty bathtub ring as high as my shoulders. Thank God, the river's gone down. It's never gotten this high before or this muddy." She stood in her kitchen the mud covering her jeans.

"I know darlin', it's terrible. Watch where you step; water's everywhere."

"Well, if you'd put down that damn shotgun and help me, we'd all be better off, ya hear?"

"I hear ya. Take my hand, Louise." They tread carefully in the slippery muck.

"Why d'ya bring that shotgun anyway?"

"Well, this is our home and I wanna make damn sure nobody comes here to loot anything. Although, lookin' at this place who would want sixty tons of muck?"

The Mississippi River ran rough at their front door. They heard the angry sounds of the rushing river and the banging of their motor boat tied up to what was left of their front porch.

"You know, Jake, I can't even see my shoes when I walk in my own living room. The mud is so deep, and it just grabs everything. Now look my shoe is stuck again."

"Here, let me help you." The thick grey-brown mud sucked her shoe under with a loud sucking noise. The putrid stench of garbage and random debris left behind in the wake of the angry river-filled the room.

"And look at this living room, Jake, the sideboard my mother gave me and the kitchen set your daddy made, all destroyed and there's a big ol' pine branch pokin' through our front window. Whatta' we gonna do?"

"We'll rebuild, like before. Like always. It'll be okay, Lou. I'll make it like new, I promise."

"I remember just a few months ago, at Christmas and you were rollin' on the floor with the kids and our new grandchil' and we were so proud of our new carpet. Now it's under three inches of water and eight inches of mud. I can't take any more of this. Maybe we should move away from the river?"

He stood tall with his head erect, "We're stayin,' Lou, this is our home. We'll get new carpet, and come summertime we'll have a grand Fourth of July party and then we'll have our usual Thanksgiving dinner with all the fixin's right here, in our home." She stood taller.

"Look, my brand-new fridge has mud up to the freezer.

"I'll get you a new one Lou."

"You sure are taking this pretty calm Jake."

"Guess it's shock, Lou, but we still got each other, and we're still alive. We got out in just the nick of time. I am thankful for that; everything else can be replaced."

"Maybe we should try to... what was that?" She heard a loud hissing noise and saw a mass of movement in the only dry spot in the dark corner of their kitchen across from where they were standing.

"What?"

"I heard something move over there by the fridge, what is it?"

He stepped toward the moving pile and then froze in place. "It's a load of snakes and look, there's more there by the kitchen door," he whispered. "Look, wow, there's dozens of them livin' in our kitchen. Theys cottonmouths, water moccasins and some rattlers and they are pissed and hungry. They must have come in here to find somewhere dry. Step back to the living room Lou, real slow-like." They retreated to their watery front room.

"That was too close for comfort," he said with a sigh.

"Jake look, look there, our wedding album is floating in the water. Oh Jake, I don't know how much more of this I can take. I think it's time to get the boat and... now what's that noise?"

"What noise?"

"There...that noise." They were both startled as they heard the clomp of heavy work boots coming down the steps.

"Yeah, somebody's coming Lou!"

They saw feet coming down from upstairs and made their way to the landing. He stopped on the stairs and managed a grin. "Howdy folks, I'm just checking on the place for the sheriff." He was a tall and lanky young kid, wearing a camouflaged hunting shirt while dangling a mud-stained pillowcase from his right hand.

"Who are you?" asked Louise.

"Name is Clemson ma'am, Deputy Matt Clemson."

"You work for the Sherriff? Sherriff Dawson in Vicksburg?" asked Jake.

"Yes sir, the one and only."

"That so, huh?"

"Yep, he deputized us and asked us to make sure that everyone has left these parts. There's more floodin' comin' right for us. It ain't safe here anymore. So I am goin' to have to ask you folks to leave now, ya hear? You can join me; I have my boat in the back, outside the kitchen."

"Well Deputy, did you know that there ain't no Sheriff Dawson in Vicksburg?"

"Well maybe, I just don't remember his name right, that's all. Now I gotta get goin'."

"Whatcha got in that pillowcase, Deputy?" asked a now very suspicious Jake.

"Just somethin' to eat, ya know."

"Why is it so noisy? Sounds like my wife's silverware.

"Oh no, not my silverware. Oh Jake, make him put it back!"

"You're not really a deputy now are you? Put that bag down now, Buddy, or I'll kick your ass into next week, you hear me! Those are our things you're stealin'!"

"No farm boy, I'm not a deputy, and you keep your hands where I can see 'em and away from that shotgun, ya hear? Don't make me use this pistol. I got it aimed right for your pretty little lady, boy. You understand me you dumb sharecropper?"

"I hear you, I ain't happy, but I understand. I understand real good. You just better not turn your back on me, son."

"Now move away, I'm comin' through and heading out the kitchen to get in my boat, you got that?"

"You can't go through the kitchen."

"You watch me pretty lady, you just watch me."

"But it's not safe."

"He's got a gun, Louise, he'll be just fine. Let's go out the front door and get outta' here."

"Bye folks, thanks for the donations… ha, ha, ha!"

"Come on Louise, we'll be back later to rebuild, just like always."

"Got to go now, bye folks," he headed for the kitchen sloshing through four inches of muddy river water.

"Bye, Deputy."

"Oh no, oh my god no, snakes, no, help, help me! Snakes! Snakes, sna…"

He helped her into the rocking boat. "You told him not to go in the kitchen. Come on now, we'll be back when the water settles down."

# Love Letters

(an excerpt)
If you found a love letter in an old book, would you read it?

Katherine Kosgrove locked the front door of her secondhand bookstore and pushed the large boxes of books over to the sofa in front of the fireplace. She made herself comfortable, sitting back with a large glass of wine, with music playing in the background and her cat Felix snuggling beside her. Katie had saved Felix from certain death at an animal shelter in Boca Raton. Apparently, nobody else wanted a one-eyed cat, but he was her buddy. Independent as hell, like her, but her buddy nonetheless.

Even though it was late, she began to search through the boxes of books she had purchased at the flea market that day. She needed to catalog her new purchases for tomorrow. Felix purred for more food but soon dozed off to sleep. Katie had to be ready for her regular, early Monday morning customers, who would be eager to search through any new books she placed on her "Just Arrived" rack.

While sorting through the first box, she could not help but be reminded of the ruggedly handsome doctor at the flea market who sold them to her. He said his name was Jack and that he was downsizing to a smaller house because his wife had recently passed away. He told her the books belonged to his wife.

The used bookstore, aptly named Secondhand Rose, was housed in a former two-story general store. The main floor downstairs was her bookstore, and the second floor was her apartment. The place had tons of space and the rent was cheap—perfect for her needs. At the rear of the store was an old, rustic stone fireplace. Katie made this area cozy and inviting for her customers. Bookshelves lined the walls, and a sofa faced the working fireplace. It wasn't just pretty, it was functional as well.

Katie's customers could peruse the books they were considering buying or wait out any of the frequent Florida rainstorms; drinking Katie's freshly brewed Tandian orange tea.

She would sometimes light the fire during the rare, cool Florida winter days, when the air became slightly chilly. Sitting there on the sofa, she could still smell the woodsy smoke from the last time the flames burned the old wood on the steel grate. But most of all, Katie enjoyed the stack of white birch logs she usually left on the open grate. They reminded her of home, and the sofa made an inviting and comfortable place to curl up with a good book.

She sorted through the first box, taking the books out and arranging them by category, condition, and genre. The first box was mainly romance novels, which were her customers' favorites. She found paperbacks written by authors such as Jackie Steil, Robin Macy, Nicholas Sparks, Maureen Hare, Nora Roberts, and Francesca Delarina, among countless others.

There was poetry by Keats, Browning, Frost, and a hardback book of poetry by an unfamiliar poet named Allison White, a book she found buried in the bottom of the box. She placed it in her own personal "to be read" pile.

Katie started forming other piles and was nearly done with the first box when she found the classic *Rebecca* by Daphne du Maurier, the twisted classic love story her mother enjoyed reading. Her mother loved it so much she had wanted to name her daughter either Rebecca or Daphne, but Katie's father would have none of it. Instead, she was named Katherine, after her paternal grandmother.

Her mother, the ballet dancer Roberta Casina, grew up outside the town of Big Sky, Wyoming, on a large cattle ranch, and spent any of her idle time reading. Katie went back to the ranch many times with her mother when her parents fought. She loved its wide-open spaces and undisturbed view of the heavenly stars. The ranch was sold at her father's insistence when he ran into financial troubles. Her mother never said a word about it, but Katie always knew she always resented the loss. The last time Katie was there was to scatter her mother's ashes across the wildflower fields.

Looking further she came across her favorite, *Wuthering Heights*, by Charlotte Brontë . "Heathcliff," she murmured aloud, her voice emulating the tone of the novel. "Heathcliff," she sighed again, the sound of an impassioned memory, causing Felix to raise his sleepy head and glance at her.

"Go back to sleep," she said to her feline fur ball, caressing his forehead. "Back, back to sleep, back to sleep," she soothed, and he was soon purring again, dreaming whatever it was that cats dreamt.

Her mind wandered back to the man at the flea market who had sold her the books. He reminded her of some Hollywood movie star, rugged good looks, tall, with broad shoulders and an easy smile. He was the type you would recognize in an instant but could not place his name.

She glanced through the classic Brontë novel, and even though she'd read it countless times, she always found the immortal love story mesmerizing. She smiled to herself, holding the cherished book in her hand. *Jack's wife had very good taste,* she thought, tossing it onto her growing "to be read" pile.

The book bounced off the sofa and landed on the floor, and what appeared to be a handwritten note spilled out onto the carpet in front of her. Katie reached for the piece of paper lying on the floor.

She unfolded the blue-lined note paper and read the first line of the handwritten letter: *My Dearest Darling…*

Katie's eyes widened. Whoa. Oh, my God, this is a treat and a treasure. Most women don't get to read love letters, and far fewer have love letters written to them. What do we have here? Most men have trouble writing and remembering a grocery list.

She clutched the letter tightly to her chest, looking around to see if anyone saw her reading someone else's love letter. It was a reflex. *Of course there's no one here. It's one A.M. Just Felix and me.*

Katie had to know more. She glanced at the blue paper. This could be a private, personal letter, but she could not resist reading on. Her curiosity got the better of her. Felix yawned in his sleep. "I know, I know what they say curiosity has done to cats," she whispered, then began to read.

*March 2007*
*My Dearest Darling,*
*I saw a sunset today, a beautiful sunset. It reminded me of you and of us. Do you recall how we would measure our days by the sunsets we saw? We would always take the time to stop and watch them, no matter where we were.*

*Remember the orange and red sunset over the plains of the Serengeti—we held hands like school kids and drew each other close, hearing the lions roar just beyond our fires. Remember the awe-inspiring sunset on the Greek island of Petros? Do you recall the marvelous sunset from the top of the hills overlooking Molokai? Oh, that magical Hawaiian island, shrouded in rainbows every day, from the wondrous mornings until the cool nightfall. And remember the sunrises on the beach in Panama? But the ones I recall most fondly were the morning sunrises on the beach of Islamorada in the Keys. It was always enough to take my breath away, as long as I was there with you, my love.*

*Breathtaking! The simple, silent beauty. There is nothing on earth like it, and to spend it with you was gold.*

*My favorite sunset of all time was on our cruise. We were dining on board, sailing the blue-green waters of the Caribbean. From our table, we could faintly see the soft, yellow rays of the setting sun. Together, we grabbed our champagne glasses and left our dinner to be alone. We watched the most gorgeous sunset of all. I cherish times such as those, my love.*

*Every time I see a sunset, I think of you and remember your beauty and what you mean to me. Each sunrise and sunset brings us closer together. Which sunsets do you recall as your favorite? Which sunrises do you cherish? I count the sunsets until we are together again.*

*I love you and miss you.*
*Forever,*
*Jack*

"Wow, how romantic can you get?" Katie took a large, loud gulp of wine. The letter was signed simply, *Jack*. No last name. It had to be the same good-looking Jack she bought the books from at the flea market. He must have written these letters to his wife.

That was some letter. Jack and his Dearest Darling really cared for one another. Then Katie remembered he'd told her his wife died a while back.

This fellow, Jack, he really loved her. He knew what his wife wanted. She wanted what every woman wants. Simple, really, Katie thought, we want love and happiness coupled with trust and respect. Everything else is just fluff. Nothing else matters.

She gazed at the handwritten letter she held. Why didn't he keep the letter? Maybe he didn't know it was in the book? He would most likely want it back if he knew. That she was sure of. Sort of.

I should read the letter again to see if there are any clues, like his last name or contact information, then I could return it. Yes, that's what I'll do. She reread the letter—twice. Nothing. It was a letter he wrote to someone else, and Katie had no right to read it. She refolded it and set it on the sofa next to her.

Somehow, this letter made her think about her ex-husband, Richard. He could never have written anything like this. He was incapable of that kind of passion, that kind of tenderness. Richard could never be that open or vulnerable. There was raw emotion pouring from this man's heart. Jack's wife had been a very lucky woman. The letter gave her hope that there were still some good men out there.

Reluctantly, she pushed it farther away from her. She still had two more large boxes to sort through and it was getting late. She pulled out the last book from the first box. It was a very large medical surgery book. Would any of her customers buy a medical book? She tossed it into her "miscellaneous" pile.

The large book hit the pile with a thud, rolling over on its side. Something stuck out from the bottom of the book. A bookmark? Or another love note? She retrieved the book from the pile, opened it to the marked page, and found a one-hundred-dollar bill.

Her mouth fell open in shock. What was going on here? Didn't people check these things before they brought them to a flea market? She scrambled to her knees, now determined to go through every book she had purchased at the flea market. Katie was on a mission.

She searched through all the books from the first box, examining each book, turning them upside down and shaking them to see if anything came out before moving on to the next box of books. The second and third boxes yielded more money and other letters, each written on different colored paper.

When she opened the other ones, she noticed each one had the same handwriting and signature, *Forever, Jack,* and the same opening, *My Dearest Darling*.

By the time she was finished, Katie had found in excess of three hundred dollars in cash and over thirty love letters. She could not believe all the money she had found, but even so, the letters were more precious than money.

Katie sat there, with her found money in one hand and the love letters in the other. She took the bills and put them into a plain white envelope, and after sealing it, she wrote on the outside of the envelope one word: *Jack*. She tucked it inside her cash register.

She sat down, made herself comfortable, and took a deep breath. She found she was unable to move, holding the treasured stack of correspondence close to her heart. She had read only one completely through, but she felt something happening inside of her, inside her heart. Something good.

Why didn't he just send his wife an email? A handwritten letter was more romantic, she argued with herself, but an email would get there faster.

Katie arranged the letters by date, starting with the first one, dated February 2007. It was then she noticed that they all only included the month and year at the top of the page. Picking up another one, she realized the first letter she had read was actually the second one he wrote.

Should she read them all now or ration them, like she did with chocolates? Or should she just bundle them away? She took another large sip of wine and settled in to read.

Since the first one I read didn't contain any contact information, maybe the next one will help me find out more about him so I can return these letters, she reasoned.

Katie paused for a moment, but try as she might, she could not stop reading. She reached for another, then another. She felt urged on.

*February 2007*
*My Dearest Darling,*
*I miss you. Some feelings are expressed so simply. This separation is beyond my control, for you know if it were in my power, I would be there by your side. This journey will take time. Time that I know cannot be replaced. Like the sands of an hourglass, one grain at a time, it drops away, silently but evermore, never to be found again. I will write you. Be comforted by the fact you will always be in my thoughts…*

*Remember, just a short few weeks ago, we celebrated New Year's Eve at the Grand Gala at the Club. You looked breathtaking in your shimmering evening gown, and I know you loved me in my tux as we moved around the dance floor. I love dancing with you. We both agreed those dance lessons certainly paid off, as we spiraled the waltz together, moved to the beat of the samba and the cha cha, and set the dance floor afire with the closeness of our tango. The thunderous applause was always for you, your beauty and grace.*

*Then the band had to play your favorite song, "MacArthur Park," and you looked at me, grabbed my hand and the champagne, and we rushed to the beach to welcome in the New Year. Your gown and my shoes were ruined from the choppy waves, but it was a New Year's Eve we will never forget. I hate the beach, but it was still the best way to celebrate the New Year. We always believed that how you spend New Year's Eve is how you spend the rest of the year. Not this year, I am afraid, my love. I love you, my dearest, always remember that. Must go.*

*Forever,*
*Jack*

She studied the intimate correspondence, which spoke so eloquently to the love he obviously felt for his wife. Katie held it to her chest and took a deep breath, but so far, she was no closer to finding out anything more about him. He had said he belonged to some club. What was the name of that club? She looked again. No luck.

Where was he writing from? Why was he writing? Why didn't he just go to her? Or call her? Was he in the navy? In Africa? Why couldn't he call her or say anything about where he was? Maybe he was on a secret spy mission and was sworn not to speak about it? But he was so handsome and seemed so honest. Maybe he was in jail? He didn't look like a jailbird, though.

His letters sounded as if he could write volumes to this woman he loved. Katie refolded the letter on her lap. She read February and March and now held April in her hands. No, these letters were too private. *They were not written to me. I am returning them tomorrow,* she told herself. *Yes, first thing tomorrow. I will call the people who run the flea market and get his address from them.* She smiled. It would be good to see him again.

April's letter was still in her hand; she caressed it with her fingers. She was surrounded by piles of books on the floor, and the precious letters were piled on top of her as she lay on her sofa. Katie took another sip of wine, stroked the soft hair on Felix's back, and thought about her wonderful day with the letter slipping from her hand. Her dreams swept her away into a land of love. A land she desperately wanted to visit. A place where she could fall in love again.

---

Katie was awakened by a loud, metallic tapping sound. *Tap, tap, tap.* She opened her eyes and found herself still lying on the sofa where she had fallen asleep the night before, right in front of the fireplace with the letters piled high on top of her. She had slept through the night—her first night without her horrible nightmare. The tapping began again. She looked at her watch: seven forty-five A.M.

She picked herself up and looked over the sofa. She heard the noise again. It was Donna McIntyre, always her first, and best, Monday morning customer. Donna wanted to be there bright and early so she could be first to peruse any new inventory.

Katie dragged herself from the sofa and unlocked the front door, then opened it, causing the door chime to ring.

"Morning, Kate, did you hear the news? They got him! They got the terrorist, *Numero Uno*! They sent in a SEAL team after locating him in Pakistan. Can you believe it? He was in Pakistan? Just where they thought he was all along. He was living in some big mansion. Go figure."

Kate moaned a sleepy reply to her loquacious customer.

"Got any good stuff? Any new books? Any new Nicholas Sparks or Nora Roberts books?" Donna asked changing the conversation. The former school principal loved to thumb through books and would usually buy three to six at a time, sometimes more.

Donna was tall and thin and looked just like the principal, Mrs. Moransky, at Katie's grade school. She always wore a long black dress, even in the hot Florida sun. Her glasses were perched high on her forehead, and she wore a long silk scarf around her neck. She nearly shrieked when she saw the piles of books scattered on the floor around the sofa.

"Very good," Donna said to no one in particular. She grabbed a number of books and plopped down on the comfy sofa, lost to the world.

Katie looked through the large front windows and noticed that for some reason the store seemed particularly dark and dreary, even though the Florida sun shone bright. She tucked all of the letters into the side pocket of her wrinkled sweatshirt, examining the store and her longtime customer.

"Make yourself comfortable, Donna. I think I am going to take down these old drapes in the front, so it may get a little dusty in here. The place looks so dark."

"You know, you are right. I never noticed it before." Donna looked up from her growing stack of books on the floor next to the sofa including her sought after Nicholas Sparks and Nora Roberts novels.

A vision of bright light soon engulfed the shop.

"Wow, what a difference!" Donna said, when the huge green velour drapes came crashing down in a pile of dust.

Katie stood and admired her handiwork but then groaned when it became apparent that the sunlight had exposed smudged, dirty windows. "Time for a bucket of water, some rags, and Windex," she said to herself, as Donna was again engrossed in her own little book world.

When Katie was done, the store was bright and airy. The front of the store shone like never before. She'd need to put some new plants in the front windows, she thought. She stood back by the sofa and breathed a deep sigh.

Her gaze fell on the small pile of medical books from the flea market. She picked them up and placed them on a shelf near the front of the store. She was not going to buy them, but at the last moment figured, what the heck? Her customers were always surprising her as to what they would and would not buy. On top of the shelf, she prominently displayed the largest and thickest book, titled *The Surgeon's Guide to Thoracic and Cardiovascular Surgery*.

"There you go, Jack," she said to the black-and-green book. "See, even if you are not here, I can still talk to you. You can be my Wilson," she said, thinking of the movie *Cast Away* with Tom Hanks. The book became her inanimate friend and confidant.

"I'm sorry, Katie, did you say something to me?"

"No, I was just thinking out loud. I do that a lot. Donna, I'm going upstairs to take a shower and will be back down soon. If you find anything you like, you know the drill; just leave the money on the register."

"Sure. Take your time. I'll keep an eye on things for you here."

"Hey, Donna, I have a question for you."

"Sure," she said, without even looking up from her new hoard of books. "Fire away."

"If you found a love letter in an old book, would you read it?"

"Of course! But I wouldn't know it was a love letter until I started reading it, you see. And besides, maybe it would have the person's address inside. Then I would know where to return it. But I would also be curious as hell. Why? Are there any love letters in here?" she asked expectantly, finally looking up from her books.

"No. No, there weren't any."

The door chimes sounded again as the front door opened, and they both looked up to see one of Katie's strangest customers, Sidney, walk through the door. He was a fixture in Delray, another one of the quirky things about the small town that always amused Katie.

But looking at him in her shop always gave Katie chills. He wore the same clothes every time she saw him, torn and tattered and with an old baseball cap covering his balding head. He always came in, asked for certain books, and then, not finding them, would turn and leave. *Strange dude with a peculiar homeless smell indeed,* Katie mused to herself. Some customers she could just do without. Once, she was pretty certain he'd followed one of her customers down the street. Katie thought he was just coming into her store to see her. He was definitely a strange dude.

"Morning," he mumbled to both of them. "Get any Raymond Chandler books in, Miss Kate?" His voice was slurred, making it sound more like an accusation than a question.

"No, Sidney. No Raymond Chandler books today. Sorry." If she ever found any at a flea market she would not buy them, fearing it would keep him coming back for more, but he never got the hint and kept coming back anyway.

He glanced at her, his dark, brooding eyes chilling the room. He looked at them both for much too long, not saying a word, before turning and leaving without so much as a goodbye.

Once he was gone, Donna shivered before saying, "Now there goes a mass murderer. But that's just my opinion," she quickly added.

"Yes, but so far he's been harmless," said Katie, trying to calm her down.

"Yeah, they say they are all like that and you never know what they are really thinking until something clicks inside their head and then boom, they explode. By then it's too late. Do you keep a gun in here, Kate?"

"No, I don't. Hey listen, I'll be back in a little while. I am just going upstairs for a bit. If you leave before I get back down, just leave me a note with how many books you left with, okay?"

"Sure, Katie. No problem."

Katie clutched all of the letters and headed upstairs. With a sigh, she sat down on her bed, laying the letters down beside her, anxious to read more. Felix came out from his secret space underneath the bed and slid next to her, purring and rubbing against her. Reading the letters was becoming addictive, but she needed to know what was in them even though it was a one-way conversation. Maybe she could just read one more while the water heated for her shower.

*April 2007*
*My Dearest Darling, I have tried to...*

*Read more of the novel Love Letter – available wherever fine books are sold.*

# The Negotiator

It was in my final year at Harvard Business School that the question was posed to the senior class: *Who is the best negotiator you have ever seen?*

Hands were raised high, and names like J.P. Morgan, Donald Trump, Andrew Carnegie, Conrad Hilton filled the air. When the initial rush of nominations was over, the long-tenured professor, Sir Winston Masters, bowed his head to look through the top of his spectacles when his eyes chose me as his target. "Ms. Johnson, would you care to add to this discussion?"

"Yes, sir," I said standing. "The best negotiator I have ever seen is a lady by the name of Agnes Wsynowski."

The class broke out in laughter and catcalls at the mention of this unknown woman vying for honors against the likes of the titans of industry.

"I am not familiar with this woman. Tell me Ms. Johnson, is she a CEO at a Fortune 500 company?"

"No sir, she is not."

"Does she head a high-tech company?"

"No sir, she does not."

"Well, tell me Ms. Johnson, is she the head of state of some small country?" His impatient voice was beginning to betray his feelings. He was not going to spar with me.

"No sir, she is not."

"So who is this woman called Agnes Wsynowski…, Ms. Johnson?" he asked leaning against his podium.

"She was my grandmother, sir."

Once again, the room was filled with cheering, laughing, and clapping at my response. The professor was fuming but I, the upstart student stood tall and straight.

"Ms. Johnson, what makes you think she is the best negotiator you have ever seen."

"The basis of negotiating is to get what you want."

"And how did she do that? Give us an example, if you please."

"My grandmother came from the old country, sir. She was not very well educated. She was a small woman, four-foot nine and weighed less than ninety pounds. She did not speak the best English, but she knew how to negotiate to get what she wanted."

"Yes," asked the professor impatiently, "…and?"

"Well every year she would have many different coal sellers knock on the door to her small home in the city and negotiate to sell her coal for the winter. She would always tell them the most she could afford to pay was .50 cents per yard. They would always try to take advantage of her because she was an immigrant and wanted to charge her $1 per yard." The young woman looked around the classroom before she continued.

"They would spend the whole day filling her coal bin, shovelful by shovelful until it could hold no more. When the sun went down and they were finished, the men, exhausted and covered with dark coal dust, would come to her to be paid. She would hand them .50 cents a yard. They would try to bully her and demand $1 per yard. When she refused they stomped their feet with their black dust filling the air before settling around them on the sidewalk."

"So how was this classic impasse negotiation settled, Ms. Johnson," asked the smug but now alert professor.

"When they continued their demands she would take her money back and told them to haul the coal away because it was too expensive. The negotiating lessons learned from this are many, but what I learned from this was… never negotiate with an old Polish woman spending her own money. You can never win."

# A New Beginning

The extra chair stood silent at the head of the table, empty, as the assembled group began to sing.

Happy birthday to you, happy birthday to you, happy birthday dear Christine, happy birthday to you.

Christine stood teary-eyed, looking around her dining room table. All of her closest friends were there, those who meant anything at all to her had come to help celebrate her fortieth birthday.

Her mom, her daughter, her sister, and her best friend Trish were all in attendance to help her celebrate. Trish had even baked a cake and added four flaming candles to the top of it.

"Make a wish," they all yelled at the same time.

She held out her arms, reaching for her three-year-old daughter Amber. "Come here sweetie," she said. She looked just like her mother, with her long blonde hair, bright green eyes, high cheekbones, and that adorable smile. "Come on now. Help Mommy blow out the candles."

The little princess relished the attention and starring role she was thrust into but more than that, she was so happy to see her mom smile again. She hugged her tight before climbing up on her lap to blow out the candles.

"Make a wish," Chrissie whispered into her ear.

The little girl glanced at the empty chair at the end of the table then squeezed her eyes tight. She opened them and quickly blew out the candles in one big breath. "Happy birthday, Mommy! I made a special wish. Can I help you open your presents? Can I? Can I? Please?"

"Yes but only after we clean up and have some cake, okay baby?"

She smiled and hugged her daughter, a hug lasting longer than usual. They had a lot more to celebrate than just the passage of time until another birthday. Christine was bursting to tell everyone the good news.

Stephanie, Christine's mom, the matriarch of the family, rose from the table and proclaimed, "Here's to my daughter, Christine," she said raising a glass of wine to toast her offspring, "and of course to my sweet Amber."

The little girl clapped her hands together and sported a broad smile. Her mom winked at her and said, "Chrissie, you don't look a day over thirty, although I must say I am still trying to get used to your shorter hairstyle. But all in all, I like it, it suits you."

Chrissie raised a glass of ice water and toasted the other three wine glasses saying, "Cheers! It has been a tough two years for me and for the baby but I couldn't have done this without all of your help and support. You were there for me when I needed you. You were there in the middle of the night when I needed a shoulder to cry on," she smiled at Trish. "You helped me with Amber. You gave me help with job interviews, but most importantly you were there with encouragement and support. I can't thank all of you enough."

One seat was empty at the head of table with no place setting before it but everyone there knew who used to sit there, but no one but her sister Janie dared to say a word.

Her sister stood across from her and joked "See Chrissie, I told you, you didn't need no man in your life. You're better off without that beer guzzlin' bum anyway."

Chrissie's eyes flashed a warning to her younger sister. She loved her dearly, but her sibling always said exactly what she was thinking without worrying about the consequences to anyone else.

"You may be right Janie, but he is still the father of my child and that is one thing that none of us can change. So please let's not mention that again when she's present. Okay?"

The words stabbed her like a knife. Silence hung in the air. Janie came to her sister's side, hugged her close and whispered in her ear, "I'm sorry. I don't know what I was thinking. Forgive me?"

Chrissie, the kind sweet soul she was, was never angry with anyone for long, especially her only sister. She looked at her, smiled, and kissed her cheek. "Of course, I'm not mad at you." There was an awkward silence.

Turning away, the birthday girl broke the quiet, tapping her glass with a spoon, announcing, "I have something I want to share with everyone." She reached into the rear pocket of her jeans and pulled out two pieces of paper and with great flourish unfolded them and began to read. "Listen up, everybody.

*"Dear Ms. Carter:*

*We are pleased to announce that you have completed all the requirements necessary for the program you were attending and it is with great pleasure we would like to award you with your General Education Development Certificate (GED). Congratulations on a job well-done!*

*John Dwyer,*
*County Director of Adult Education*

The air was filled with clapping and whistles while everyone rushed to congratulate her.

"Wait, wait there's more. Sit, please everyone please sit down."

Her little one hugged her leg and then sat down next to her.

She stood facing her friends and family as if she was making an official announcement. She paused, savoring the moment, and then she began to read from the other sheet of paper.

*"Dear Ms. Carter:*

*This is to inform you that after a thorough evaluation by our review committee, our editorial staff, and the executive board of Brewster Press we are pleased to announce that we have accepted your children's book, Amber and Me for immediate publication. Please find enclosed an advance check for $4,000 and the appropriate contracts for you to sign. Thank you for considering Brewster Press and we look forward to a long and continued relationship and anxiously await your next promised manuscript.*

*Sincerely,*
*Linda Roots*
*Acquisitions Director*
*Brewster Press"*

She held up the check for all to see, with a smile the size of the Grand Canyon blossoming on her face. "Now I can finally pay back some of the money that you all have lent me. I don't know how to thank you all, I really don't." Her voice quivered, and tears began to swell in her eyes. Her mother was crying, so was Janie. Trish was searching for her camera, as usual. The phone in the kitchen rang and Chrissie said, "Saved by the bell! Be right back."

She picked up the phone. "Hello?" she said.

"Hey baby, happy birthday."

Her knees shook, she swallowed hard at hearing his voice, the voice she had not heard in two years. She could not talk; she swallowed again, finally saying, "Hi Jimmy."

"Sorry I couldn't be there. I've missed you a lot."

"Yeah, I've missed you too." She sat down on a kitchen chair unable to stand any longer.

"I got you a present. Not much, but I think you'll like it."

"Yeah, that's nice," she said, pressing the phone closer to her lips.

"I hear a party in the background. Is that the gang?"

"No. I haven't seen them at all, at least not for over a year or so. It's my mom, my sister Janie, Amber, and Trish."

"Your mom? What's she doing there? I didn't think you two got along."

"We do now. We patched things up. She has been a big help to me and the baby."

Changing the subject, she asked him, "Jimmy, do you want to talk to your daughter Amber? It's been quite a while."

"No, I'm sure she hates me."

"No Jimmy..., she doesn't hate you. Wait let me get her. Amber? Amber? Come in here sweetheart, your daddy's on the line and wants to say hello."

The voices in the other room had become silent at the mention of his name.

She stood and saw her daughter sitting on the floor, trembling, hiding from her and from him. Her grandmother stood next to the quivering toddler, shaking her head no.

"She must be taking a nap."

"That's okay, Chrissie, some other time maybe."

"Yeah, sure."

"Hey, if you can break away from your party why don't you come on over. I'm stayin' at Stevie's place. I can give you your present, and we can talk and ...and you know...we'll see what happens."

She squirmed in her chair. It had been two years, maybe longer. She heard him continue to talk. One phone call, the sound of his voice then visualizing his face on the end of the line is all it took. Strange the hold he had on her. She could not help it. She listened to the words he was saying as he continued to ramble. It was then she realized, nothing had changed. It was as if someone had slapped her across the face. She stopped squirming.

Something snapped inside her head, and Chrissie thought about everything she had accomplished over the past two years as she looked in the other room and saw her mom, her daughter, her sister, and her best friend busying themselves cleaning up the dishes. She had put them through a lot.

He continued to talk, but he thought he was talking to the old Christine. Six months ago his words would have melted her heart but this was the new Chrissie. One with responsibilities, a future, and a life filled with people who loved her and care for her. A life she had worked hard to create and one she was not about to give up. She turned her attention back to the phone. She had choices to make.

"And hey, baby, if you can pick up some beer and a couple of pizzas for me and Stevie and the guys that would be great. What do you say, baby?"

He was still the same old Jimmy, only thinking of himself and still the ultimate user.

"No Jimmy, I don't think so but thanks for callin.' I'm havin' a party here with all my friends and I gotta go. Good talkin' to ya. Bye Jimmy."

Janie was right; I don't need no man, at least not this one. She hung up the phone and hollered into the other room, "Who wants some birthday cake?"

# Fitz

Brian Fitzgerald, "Fitz" to all who knew him, was thirty-nine years old, and he had traveled the world for what seemed his whole life. His soul would get wanderlust any time he found himself in one place for too long. He was always anxious to see the horizon over the next hill and discover new people and new places.

Brian attended the University of the World and learned from the school of hard knocks. He was a free spirit who loved the traveling life and the scores of friends he made along the way but at the same time missed his family back home in Illinois, they called him the "wanderer."

Even as a child, he had the casual grace of a prince, the sexy good looks of Tom Cruise and that wonderful Robert Redford smile of his. He could warm the winter frost with that smile.

"Fitz" grew up in a small village hamlet named Elsah, Illinois, near the confluence of the meandering Missouri River, the mighty Mississippi, and the headstrong Illinois River. He loved exploring their secluded caves, which pocketed the great river road. Every spring as a teenager, he sketched and photographed the wild bald eagles as they annually migrated home to the valley of the rivers to mate and build their nests.

Growing older he spent time in the fair city of Seattle where her tears kept him warm and safe. It was another place he called home. Dublin was his heartthrob with its kindhearted people, late pub nights, cool winters, friendly people, and the familiar ancient yore of the Gaelic tongue to keep his devilish eyes twinkling. And Paris…, ah yes Paris, she held his heart, but it was not to be for he loved her, but when he returned she said no. His heart ached, but his feet moved him to travel onward, never to return his bleeding heart to the city of light.

It was a warm June late afternoon when his old borrowed Land Rover finally gave out with a clunk and then hiss of steam rising from underneath the hood of the car on a two-lane road outside of Missoula Montana. He was on his way to California via Seattle with a detour through Portland Oregon. He grabbed his old leather shoulder bag, his pipe, and his ever-present cache of books and walked the three miles into town. As he walked along the main street, he put coins into out-of-time parking meters. Nobody should have to pay for a space on God's good earth he always reasoned.

A blinking neon Guinness Beer sign beckoned him inside the Blackfoot Irish Pub; it was his kind of place. The cool air refreshed him, and he saw an old six-string guitar in the corner next to a stool on the stage. A waitress looked up and smiled before looking back down again cleaning her beer glasses. She smiled a sweet smile but only for tips.

"What can I get you," she finally asked, wiping the aged bar top with her old rag.

"A tall, cool pint of Guinness sounds good," he said with a smile.

"Okay," she said, pouring the beer while she watched the brown and black froth slide down the side of the glass. "You know in Ireland they serve it warm," she said waiting for the beer to settle.

"Yeah, I know," he said still eyeing the guitar.

"You been there? To Ireland?" she asked, now suddenly interested.

"Yeah, many times. I lived there for a while. It is the nearest side of heaven."

Her smile was genuine now as she placed the beer mug in front of him. He took a long slow drink and breathed in deep. He finished it on the second swig.

"Another?"

"Sure, why not. Hey, do you think anyone would mind if I strummed that guitar a bit? I promise to be careful."

"It's my bar and my guitar. My name is May, May Malone. Go at it. Maybe do an Irish rover tune or... Danny Boy?"

He smiled his trademark smile and grabbed the second beer as he made his way to the stage. The guitar showed its aged with use but it felt comfortable on his knee and around his shoulder as he struck a chord, then another. He tightened the guitar strings, strummed once more, and then tried again. On the third time, it sang sweet. A young couple walked inside and sat down at one of the tables. Then an old man in jeans sat at the bar and ordered a drink.

The waitress brought him another beer. He smiled, strummed his guitar, and began to play. He sang, soft and slow,

*Oh Danny boy, the pipes, the pipes are
calling
From glen to glen, and down the mountain
side...*

His sweet voice curled through the small out of the way bar and charmed those who filed in to listen to the sounds of the young troubadour. For hours, he played song after song to a now packed audience and listened to their generous applause.

At closing time she whispered to him when she brought him another Guinness, "Fitz, how about a Harry Chapin song for the finale?"

A smile covered his face. "He's my favorite."

The young minstrel positioned the guitar across on his knee. "I would like to dedicate this to May, thanks for the hospitality. My last song is a Harry Chapin song called, *A Better Place to Be*. He began to sing so sweetly.

*She was there in the early morning barroom…*

He had caught their souls and they joined him in his journey to nowhere. He looked around the room filled with new friends as he finished singing the song,

*… a better place to be.*

That night she took him to her home and to her bosom.

The next day she arranged for his Land Rover be towed to the local garage to begin the long process of fixing the ancient foreign vehicle. She took him to the wild sonnet flower fields where he sketched her naked while she daydreamed under the warm Montana sky. They made love in the blossoming fields. Later he asked her, "What brought you to Montana?"

She smiled that sweet smile of hers and said, "My car broke down on my way back east."

"Really?" he said. Now it was his turn to be amused. "And…?"

"Well, while my car was getting fixed, I met a guy who owned a bar. We got married, but then he left me. So I kept the bar and he kept the waitress." They both laughed. "So I never got back east."

"What's back east?"

"I was on my way back to Nepal. I worked for a great organization that builds children's orphanages there. It is a mystical place. A city like no other place in the world and the work they do for those kids is wonderful. You would love it. You should go there some time."

He smiled at her and kissed her, but his mind was travelling the thousands of miles away to the mountains far beyond.

He left there weeks later to continue onward to California, but he could not get Nepal out of his mind.

A year later, a letter arrived at the bar in Missoula. He sent her a note that he had made it to Nepal, the rooftop of the world, and was happy building places for the children. He had found what he was looking for in his life. He wrote of how fulfilling it was building homes for the children and the plans that he made to build even more. He travelled throughout Nepal scouting for future sites to build.

It was a cool January day in Kathmandu, and a light coating of snow covered the streets the night before. Fitz was excited about his latest and biggest project. He had truly found his place in the world. He went to the balcony of a local restaurant to have a smoke from his pipe and wait for some friends to join him. When they arrived, they found him sitting in a chair with his arms folded and his glasses propped on top of his head. He had gone to sleep never to wake again. He had died from a heart condition called cardiomyopathy.

While we think of him daily as elsewhere, he is still all around us. I know because at the strangest times I sometimes hear the sweet refrain whispering in the hills, sounding so sweet:

*Oh Danny boy, the pipes, the pipes are calling…*

*In loving memory
of
Brian Fitzgerald Mooney (1969 – 2008)*

# The Perfect Baby

"I am sorry ma'am, I don't know of any other tactful way to say this, but… your baby is not what we are looking for," said the smug, skinny-bow tied judge, seated at the long conference table. Two of the other judges seated next to him nodded their heads in agreement.

Looking back at that day it had been many years since I heard those terrible words but they still ring loud in my ears. Time had hardly dulled the pain in the twenty-five years that had passed since that day, as I now sat and watched the end of the magnificent ballet, *Giselle*.

Yes. They all had smiled, that sweet gatekeeper's smile, meant to assuage me and make me feel better, to try to take the sting out of their unkind words.

"She does not have the cherub, round, sweet face of the baby we are looking for to represent us in our new Berger Baby Food campaign. Her smile does not illuminate the room; her check structure is not in balance with the rest of her body. Your baby is not in keeping with the development that we like to see. We are searching for tradition and perfection with our new Berger Baby. I am so sorry," smiling that same old hated smile again. Once more they all nodded in agreement.

"So my beautiful Maria does not meet your traditional standards? She is not in keeping with the likes of Rembrandt, Botticelli, Bronzino, or Uccello, is that what you are saying?"

"Yes ma'am, exactly," chimed in the sole female judge with her black and grey hair pulled tightly and clipped to the back of her head. She was in charge of their marketing and advertising but also served as their chief gatekeeper. "I am so glad that you understand. But we do thank you for coming in and do hope that you will continue using Berger Baby food for your sweet baby." She smiled, pursing her lips together.

"If I may be permitted to say, my baby may not be sculpted in the likes of Michelangelo, but times are changing. New worlds are challenging the old, what with the likes of Rothko, Picasso, Murano, and Warhol. Their perception of the universe and mine, is quite different from yours, it seems. Your perceptions are unfathomable, and please just bear in mind it is only a baby contest."

"Yes ma'am, but it is our contest. We sincerely appreciate your input, but we do have other parents and their babies to interview for our competition. Thank you so much for coming in."

They did find their "perfect" baby some months later. Caitlin was her name. But even their "perfect" baby could not stop the slide in sales of their baby food, as mothers sought different, healthier, and more organic foods for their young ones.

Now years later, I stood with the others in the audience to applaud the prima ballerina, Maria Contese, my daughter. She was beautiful, even though her chin was still not in ideal balance with the rest of her face, nor were her cheeks the perfect cumulus shape. But there she stood, my daughter, smiling her radiant smile, the straight-A student, the loving daughter, the devoted wife and mother, and she was still my baby, my perfect baby.

# Excuses

"You're fired!"

"What do you mean I'm fired?"

"You heard me, pack up your desk and hand over all of your sales leads, if you have any, to Delores and leave the building. Go quietly or I'll call security."

"Mona, wait, I really need this job. I have a family to support, you can't fire me."

"I just did Harry."

"Why?"

"Because you are not producing any sales, that's why."

"What do you mean?"

"Harry, I really like you, but I have a business to run, and I also have a family to support. But you are not selling anything; you just sit at your desk all day long and do nothing. It's costing me money. I could use that money for other things or to hire other people and bring more sales in to put bread on my table at home."

"But Mona..."

"No Harry, I'm tired of it. If we don't sell things here we're out of business, do you understand me, we're out of business."

"But I now have my sales routine down to a science, the perfect way to sell, just like I learned in college. It can't miss. I just needed to perfect it a little bit more. Let me show you."

Against her better judgment she responded, "Bring it in to my office in twenty minutes and lay out your can't-miss plan for me. But Harry, it had better be good. This I have to see."

Two hours later...

"Mona, are you ready for me?"

"Yeah Harry, come on in."

"Thanks for giving me this second chance Mona, you won't regret it, I promise."

"Okay, okay," she said looking at her watch and noting he was two hours late, "just show me you best stuff. What's your can't miss plan?"

"Well, I take all of the lead sheets and prospect lists that you give me and send out either an e-mail or a letter to them explaining what we do and how we can save them money and make them more efficient."

"Sounds good so far."

"I also insert my business card for their files and ask them if they have any questions to please call me."

"Well, I hope you don't wait for them to call you?"

"Oh, no! I also tell them in the letter that I'll follow-up with them in a week or so to see if they have any questions or if they would like to sit down and discuss how we can help them increase their sales."

"Outstanding! That's great! That's the initiative I liked about you when I hired you. The words of honey just flowed from your lips. What's next? When do you call them? Mondays?"

"No, Monday is the first day of the week, and nobody wants to talk to a salesman on a Monday. They are still talking about their weekend."

"You're right. Fridays? You call them on Fridays?"

"No, oh my god no. They are getting ready for the weekend, and the last thing they want to do is talk to a salesman while they are planning their weekends."

"Thursdays?"

"No, Thursdays they are planning for Friday and for the weekend."

"Harry help me here, Wednesdays?"

"No everybody knows Wednesday is hump day and no work gets done on Hump Day!"

"That leaves Tuesday. You call everybody on Tuesdays Harry, right?"

"You bet!"

"Great! Now we are getting somewhere. So you set aside all day Tuesday and do all of your follow-up calls starting the first thing Tuesday? When do you start, 8 A.M.?"

"Oh no people are just getting in to the office at eight, that's not a good time to talk to them."

"You call them at four o'clock?"

"No, at four o'clock they are looking at the clock and getting ready to head out the door to go home."

"Nine o'clock Harry? You call them at nine?"

"Oh no, from nine until ten they all are on their coffee break and you can't reach anyone between nine and ten o'clock."

"I guess then you call them at twelve o'clock Harry?"

"No, never at twelve 'cause they are all on their lunch break from twelve until two o'clock."

"What about three o'clock Harry? Do you call them at three? Please tell me you call them at three o'clock."

"No, by that time they are all on their afternoon coffee break or recuperating from lunch."

"Harry that only leaves eleven o'clock. Please, please, tell me you call them at eleven o'clock?"

"Bingo! That is the best time to call them; they are prepped and ready to hear a sales pitch."

"So why do you make so few sales Harry? What happens at eleven o'clock?"

"Oh, that's when I take my coffee break, boss, at eleven o'clock."

"What?"

"I told you it's not perfect, I'm still workin' on it."

"Harry?"

"Yeah boss?"

"You're fired."

"I figured as much."

"Goodbye, Harry."

"Bye, Mona. Oh boss can I ask a favor?"

"What is it Harry?"

"Would you mind writing a letter of recommendation for me?"

"Not at all, Harry."

"When can I come by and pick it up?"

"How about eleven o'clock on Tuesday."

# Have a Heart

"Help me! Will somebody please help me! Hello! Nurse I've been waiting here for hours."

A hospital nurse hustled forward from behind the counter, with short brown hair and an understanding smile. "Yes sir, how can I help you?" she asked, wearing a white starched nurse's uniform with the name Nurse Baldwin block stitched over her pocket in a dark green color.

"Nurse, it's my wife Carol, Caroline Myers. I brought her to the emergency room over four hours ago, and then they moved her up here to this floor. I've been waiting forever. What's going on?"

"The doctor will be right out, Mr. Myers. If you would have a seat and be patient, just a little while longer. Wait, here comes the doctor now."

"Mr. Myers, hello I'm Dr. Ling," said the balding Asian doctor with kind eyes. "Nurse Baldwin can you please go check to see if the rest of the test results for Mrs. Meyers have come back yet."

"Yes doctor," she said, hurrying down the shiny tiled hallway.

"Tell me what happened," he asked as they walked to the now-deserted waiting room with its green and white sterile tiled floor and piles of discarded newspapers stacked high on the nearby sofa.

"We were driving back from a party, and she was laughing and joking with me like always, and then the next thing I know she started coughing and her eyelids fluttered and she passed out. I pulled the car over to the side of the road, thinking she was choking on something but she came to and seemed to be fine.

"Mr. Meyer, did your wife have a lot to drink?"

"No, doctor she doesn't drink anymore, we're trying to have another baby."

"What happened next?"

"When she woke up she appeared fine but slightly disoriented. A few minutes later it happened again only this time she didn't wake up."

"Has she complained recently about anything that has been bothering her?"

"Well, she has had a persistent sore throat, she gets tired easily, and she's having constant headaches, but I thought it was from the spring pollen."

"Has she had the rash on her back long?"

"Well, yes, I guess for about two weeks."

"I had a specialist examine her, but I am reluctant to give you a prognosis at this point without doing some further tests."

"Doc, come on, you've got to help me here. What's happening to my wife? I have to know either good news or bad news but I have to know."

"Okay Mr. Myers please calm down. This is just a preliminary diagnosis and we'll know more when the test results come back. I know this is an awful time for you, but based on our findings, and mind you these are just preliminary, we feel that your wife is suffering from kidney failure which has led to a heart malfunction and to the coma."

"Doc, she's only forty-two years old, she watches what she eats, and she is always in the gym exercising. What do we do?"

"If this is indeed the case, then she will need a transplant, maybe even a multiple transplant depending how much damage there has been to her heart—and soon."

"Soon?"

"Within the next two weeks."

"A transplant in two weeks?"

"We have other tests to perform, and we should have a better understanding as to the extent of your wife's internal injuries within a day or so. For now go home and get some rest. Your wife is resting now and you both are going to need your strength. Come back here tomorrow."

"I'd like to stay here if that's okay with you, Doc."

"I really won't know anything for a couple of days."

"Can I go back and see her?"

"As soon as they move her to a permanent room, and we have all of her monitors set up. I'll have one of the nurses come out and get you."

"Thank you, doctor."

"I'm so sorry to have to deliver such news to you but hang in there, okay?"

"Yeah, whatever you say. If she needs a transplant can you perform the surgery here?"

"Let's cross that bridge when we get to it, all right?"

"Sure, but can you?"

"Mr. Myers…please, sit down. At the present time there is an eight-year waiting list for people needing a liver or kidney transplant and a ten-year waiting list of over 100,000 people waiting for a new heart."

"Can't I give her my liver or kidney?"

"We can test you for kidney compatibility, but it is highly unlikely you will be compatible."

"But we can't wait that long."

"I know. We have been trying to open up broader organ donation registration to the public using driver licenses as they do in other countries, but people resist. It's tragic."

"Doctor Ying, what are we going to do?"

"Say lots of prayers and... wait here comes Nurse Baldwin, maybe she has your wife's test results. Excuse me for a minute Mr. Myers while I talk with her."

The two white-coated health care professionals muttered in low, dark tones before the doctor rejoined the anxious husband.

"What were the test results Doctor?"

"Mr. Myers... I'm afraid I have some bad news... your wife passed away three minutes ago. They tried to revive her, but it was of no use. I am so sorry."

"What, my Caroline, gone... No, I don't..., I can't believe it. No, not my Carol... she was my best friend. She was all I had in the world. Did she wake at all? Did she ask for me?"

"No sir, she never regained consciousness. It all happened so quick. I am so sorry for your loss."

"Doc?"

"I'm sorry; I thought we had more time to make our decisions, but this is sometimes the way it happens. I'm so sorry."

The exhausted husband slumped into a nearby chair.

"Mr. Myers, I know this is a difficult time for you having just lost your wife and I hate to at this sad time, but I don't have a lot of time. Your wife had a signed organ donor card in her wallet, consenting to organ donation if she died. She wanted her organs donated to those in need."

"She did?"

"Yes Mr. Myers, she did. There are people in need just like Caroline all over the country. It could make a difference between life and death. Even though she had signed a card indicating her donor preferences, by law, if a member of the family is present, we have to ask their permission as well. Mr. Myers do we have your permission?" Silence.

"Mr.Myers?"

# Words

"I don't love you anymore," he said. The words hung in the air, seemingly floating to earth. I took it all in wondering if he was talking to me or perhaps reading from a newspaper like he always did. *Maybe it was a dream. Maybe I misunderstood.* Yes, that was it, he was saying he no longer liked the way I wore my hair. It was after midnight after all and we both had drunk a lot of wine at the party.

Then he said it again, "Did you hear me? I said I don't love you anymore. I have met someone who fulfills me."

"You mean like a balloon?" My quirky sense of humor was always getting me in trouble even at delicate times such as this. "I'm sorry, I couldn't help it." Maybe it was just another one of my defenses.

We had been married for over twenty-five years, had three wonderful grown kids, another five years on the mortgage, and talked about what we would do when we stopped working and now he was saying he was done, just like that. Throwing away our life like a used paper towel. No lead-up to it, just blurting out that he was done or at least that's what it sounded like.

I turned to him, now fully awake asking, "What do you mean?"

"I want a divorce."

"What?"

"You heard me, I want a divorce. I'll give you everything, the house, the cars, the bank account, the place at the beach, a generous settlement, alimony, and full custody but I want this whole thing over with quickly."

"What's the rush? Did you get someone pregnant?" I asked in jest.

"Yes. It's one of the girls at the office…, I love her."

"Girl? Don't you think you should wait a little bit until she's a woman?" There I went again.

"Do you really want to be changing diapers again at your age?"

"I love her, I tell you."

"You love her? What about us? I thought you loved me?" He was silent.

"Where do you intend on setting up your little love nest…, in her apartment? And what about when her old boyfriends stop by for a beer and some laughs, where are you going to sleep? How are you going to feel? Probably like I feel now."

"I love her. I'm sorry; I never meant to hurt you."

"Well, I tell you what, why don't you get your sorry ass out of here and run to your little girl. And leave your house keys on the table downstairs, you sorry sack of shit."

"I love her… blah blah blah……….." She stopped typing and looked at what she had written.

"This is not how I want to end this story. Jon…, Jonathan wake up. I need to finish this piece for my writing class tomorrow, but it just doesn't have enough oomph to it. Jon can you hear me. Come on wake up. I need your help; you're so good at things like this. Jon come on I need you."

He was snoring and never heard a word she said.

"Well, first thing tomorrow you're going to help me with this story. Do you hear me? You're always good helping me when I get stuck." She leaned over, turned off the bedside light and kissed him on the cheek, "Good night, my love." She lay back in bed, closed her eyes, and began to doze off.

His snoring stopped for a brief moment and in the silence of the room, she heard him whisper, "I love her I tell you."

# The Lemon Trees

Fergus Tucker Macgregor stood tall on the wraparound porch of the large impressive house where he and his beloved wife Eileen had been living their retirement years. They would sit for hours relaxing on the front porch swing. The stone home stood prominently at the top of the hill that overlooked the lush green valley and wide lake below.

The tranquil scene reminded them so much of their cherished Cairnwell Valley in the Scottish Highlands of Aberdeenshire that they had left behind so many years ago. It was a valley filled with the purple heather, fragrant raven's wood, and bright fields of yellow flower blossoms carpeting the valley below. To them it was a place the nearest side of heaven.

Now his Eileen was dead, gone from his life forever. She was his heart, his strength, his soul. Fergus was sure to follow her soon, for a man cannot survive in this world when one loses their lonely heart. He could not bear a life without her; he knew it was only a matter of time.

His treasured Eileen was gone, murdered. Maybe not murdered in the traditional sense but killed nonetheless. She died from a broken heart, and now he would have his revenge.

That day as the tall Scotsman overlooked his valley below; he came upon his plan for retribution. His design would take time, but with her gone the one thing he had was time. He put his plan into motion the very day of her funeral.

Fergus and Eileen Macgregor had left Scotland decades earlier to come to America for opportunity and to start a family. Shortly after their arrival, Fergus, a cobbler by trade, had set up his shop downtown in a small storefront building. He was immediately busy repairing and resoling shoes. Two years later, he bought the building.

Fergus Macgregor was a true Scotsman, a tightwad if truth be told, and he never spent a dime needlessly— he considered it a mortal sin to waste anything. The married couple lived together frugally, in the small two-bedroom apartment over his repair shop. He would come upstairs to the apartment at noon every day for the lunch that Eileen had prepared for him. At seven P.M., he would close up his shop and they would have a simple dinner together.

They were happy and prospered, while they had raised twin boys who at age nineteen enlisted in the Army together. Ian and Brent were in the same unit together and were shipped overseas. They fought in the most ferocious battle of the war and both boys died. Eileen and Fergus were devastated by the loss of their two young sons.

Eileen kept the flags the Army gave them in a glass showcase near the living room. The uniformed representatives told the grieving parents at the funeral that the flags were a gift "from a grateful nation." She would have preferred to have her boys back. Over the years, time began to heal their wounds.

Folks in town would joke that Fergus was so tight with a dollar that he would cross the street to pick up a penny. When it came to money, he was very shrewd. For years, he worked hard at his shoe repair shop and invested every dollar he made into real estate.

"You can touch it and feel the warmth of the good earth that our God has made," he would often say with a faraway look in his eyes and then he would joke, "It's a rare item. They aren't making any more of it. God is done making land for us."

He bought real estate far out in the country, he would buy land and buildings downtown, he bought acreage in the lush valleys surrounding the town, and he never sold anything he had purchased. "There will come a time when I will sell," he told his closest friends. He bought real estate and watched its value rise year after year.

He first saw the land at the lake on a bright Sunday afternoon. He and Eileen picnicked in the field above the valley that overlooked a large peaceful lake. It reminded her of her home in Scotland. "Fergus, when we retire one day," she told him, "this is where I want to build our home."

Shortly afterward, he started buying the land where they had picnicked. He bought the land in the valley, he bought the land around the lake, small pieces here, larger pieces there, until he had accumulated every parcel. He named the valley, The Cairnwell, after the Cairnwell Valley in their cherished Scottish homeland.

When Eileen finally told him one day, many years later, "Fergus we are not getting any younger, let's settle down, and build a proper home," he took her to the valley and showed her the land that he had bought for them to build their retirement home. It was the same valley where they had picnicked years earlier. She smiled at her loving husband.

When they were ready to retire, Fergus Macgregor put all of his real estate up for sale, except the Cairnwell properties. He was astonished at the amount of money that they had made on the sale of the land. One evening, a short while later, he told Eileen of the millions they had made from the sale of the properties, and she promptly fainted.

Once they retired, they built a large stone house on the crest of the hill that overlooked both the beautiful valley and the tranquil lake below. In the home that they built, in keeping with Scottish tradition, they built a massive stone fireplace in the living room. It was so large a grown man could walk inside of it without having to lean over.

The outside of the house had a large wraparound porch with a swing in the front, where he and his beloved Eileen would spend hours admiring the valley and lake below. They would often joke about the picnic that they had at that exact same spot many years earlier.

In honor of each of her sons, Eileen planted two lemon trees at the base of the hill, near the lake and named them after her sons, Ian and Brent. The trees grew tall and strong, as she had hoped her sons would have grown.

Sometimes at night, when a cool breeze was blowing off the lake, they could catch the faint scent of the sweet lemon blossoms, as it made its way up the valley and wrapped its arms around the big old house, and settled into the cozy corners of the stone home, like a welcome friend.

Fergus would always ask her, "Why do you spend money on lemon trees? Why not plant apple trees? At least you could make apple pies from the apples; you can't do anything with a lemon except make lemonade." After trying lemonade for a couple of days, he soon tired of the sour drink and returned to his homemade basement brew of Scottish whiskey.

"Hush," she would always whisper solemnly to her loving husband, "you're talking about our boys out there." Eileen enjoyed picking the lemons and whispering to her boys as she placed the lemons inside her outstretched apron. Once back home in her big kitchen she would polish the bright yellow fruit and put them into a crystal bowl as a pretty centerpiece for the dining room table. It brought her comfort to have her boys so near.

After they planted the lemon trees, Fergus, in the Scottish tradition of giving back when wealth is obtained, built a small brick cottage near his home and donated the use of it, rent free, to the House of Ruth for abused women. He told them that the cottage was theirs to use for as long as they wanted. The organization renamed the small, two-bedroom cottage, The House of Macgregor.

Women, many with small children, would come in the middle of the night and stay in the cottage. Sometimes they would stay for a few weeks and other times they would stay for months before leaving. They were always thankful to the Macgregors, thankful to have a safe, warm place to sleep and get their life back in order. Many days they would leave the Macgregors presents of flowers, cookies, and the like at their doorstep, which always made Eileen and Fergus proud. Eileen would often return the kind gestures with homemade apple pies and dolls for the little ones.

Life was peaceful for many years until early one morning, bulldozers arrived at the lake property and began tearing up the hillside and building a road down the middle of the Macgregor land.

The white-haired, wiry Scotsman with an oversized shotgun in his hands stopped them. "Get off my land!" he commanded.

The developer called the county sheriff and after he produced a proper title to the land, the sheriff ordered Fergus to go home. Unfortunately, Fergus soon discovered he had been recently swindled out of his lakefront property by a crooked developer and an unsavory politician. Strangers now owned his land by the lake. He had new neighbors to share his beautiful valley with… and he was not happy.

The houses built on that land, at the bottom of the valley, around what was now called Lake Marcus, named after the builders son, were sold as fast as they were built, because everyone loved the view of the lake. They also loved the privacy, the same privacy that Fergus and Eileen had sought when they built their stone home.

Things were peaceful until the new neighbors started to move in with their fast laughing convertibles, big BMWs, dark Mercedes SUVs, and oversized trucks and they began racing on the road beside the Macgregor property. They threw parties at the lake lasting sometimes until three A.M., with their vulgar sounds coming harshly up the valley and disturbing their restful sleep.

One day there was a knock at the door of the Macgregor home and when the old Scotsman opened it, two of the newest lakeside residents stood before him.

"Hi neighbor," said the perky little wife, wearing flip-flops and a tight top and he with his white polo shirt, one with a collar that stayed up as if it had been starched to remain that way.

They continued in their annoying little voices, "Mr. Macgregor, we have a request for you from your neighbors down by the lake. Is it all right for us to remove those nasty lemon trees at the bottom of the hill? The smell from the flowers is awful, and the lemon fruit litters the road and the juice gets all over our tires. You don't mind do you?"

Old man Macgregor stood tall before them, hovering like the immense Scottish mountains with a terrific storm brewing, as he marched slowly towards the two saying, "You want to cut down my boys?" He approached them closer on the porch. They backed away from the crazy Scotsman.

He continued advancing, "You want to cut down the boys we raised, nurtured, and watch grow strong. My boys? Is that what you are asking?" his voice rising to a fever pitch. The storm dissipated in an instant with words emanating from inside the house, "Fergus… come finish your supper," she said gently.

"No, you may not chop down those trees." He replied to the cowering supplicants before him, "They are on my land, leave them alone. Better yet, just leave," said the elder Macgregor gruffly, slammed the door in their face and returned to his meal.

Two weeks later the first of the trees, Ian, died and all the grass around it turned brown, apparently, someone had poured gasoline at the base of tree. In the middle of the night, three days later, someone cut down the other tree, named Brent, waking only Scottie, their twelve-year-old, nearly blind Scottish terrier.

It was the end for Eileen, her peace and quiet now gone, her boys killed once again, and there was nothing she could do about it. Eileen passed away three months later. The only local who came to the funeral was a woman named Sarah Anderson and her three-year-old Cheshire cat. The black and white cat laid down on the floor of the funeral parlor and promptly fell asleep. Sarah was the latest occupant at the Macgregor House for Women.

"I am so sorry for your loss," she whispered to old man Macgregor.

His once twinkling eyes now dark from grief, his loud clear voice now muffled, as he responded, "Thank you Sarah."

"Your wife was always so kind, with a wave here, a smile there. I always enjoyed her rhubarb pie that she would leave on my doorstep. I am so sorry, I will miss her." She turned and walked away, as she bowed her head in prayer. Sarah placed a small bouquet of flowers on top of the coffin with a simple note that said, "Goodbye, Eileen. You will be missed—Your Friend, Sarah."

Eileen Helena Macgregor was laid to rest in a small plot of land near the house she loved, under the arms of a huge comforting sycamore tree.

Fergus Macgregor now stood on his porch, with his beloved Eileen gone. His life was empty and a small tear struggled down his time worn face, making a trail through the dusty crevices of his countenance before ending at his thick, bushy grey mustache. He always thought that in America if you did good and lived a good life that life would be good for you… but that did not happen here with his new neighbors. He thought everyone should just get along, but it was not to be.

Standing on his front porch after her death, his dusty blue eyes twinkled that devilish smile of his as if he found the answer to a puzzling old riddle. Fergus called his attorney, James Parker the next day and arranged to meet with him for lunch. He wanted to discuss some legal matters, with the attorney paying for the meal, of course.

Six months later Macgregor joined his beloved Eileen in their graveyard plot together. Once again, they were side by side. "As in life so as in death," Fergus would always say.

Only Sarah attended the funeral. She laid a bouquet of daisies on the coffin and said her brief goodbye to Fergus Macgregor.

Shortly thereafter, an official-looking envelope arrived in the mailbox of everyone that lived around the old Scotsman's land and the return address was one of the biggest law firms in town. Inside was an invitation to the reading of the will of Mr. Fergus Tucker Macgregor, scheduled for Thursday at nine A.M. in the attorney's office.

On Thursday, all of the homeowners that lived by the lake attended. They were laughing and talking with each other, creating a carnival atmosphere, with no respect for why they were there. They had talked amongst themselves earlier and wondered what the old man wanted with them today. They were a boisterous crowd.

James Parker, Macgregor's long-time attorney, took a seat behind the long wooden conference table at the front of the room and asked for quiet.

Parker was a tall, thin, and a very distinguished looking gentleman. He had a close-cropped white beard, wore a dark navy suit, a subtle silk tie, and sported an American flag pin in the lapel of his custom tailored English suit.

Promptly at nine A.M., he began. "I am here today," he started, as the room became silent, "to make public the last will and testament of Mr. Fergus Tucker Macgregor. I would like to thank all of you for coming today."

"Is this going to take long?" asked one of the younger women, "I have a tennis game at ten-thirty."

"No, it should not take long at all. The will has two parts to it. The first item is, now that Mr. Macgregor is gone, there is no one to take care of his aging dog, Scottie. He is asking for a volunteer to take the dog and care for him in his remaining years." The room was abuzz with laughter and snickers.

"I can take him and drop him off at the pound," yelled Roberts, the oaf who drove the big Lexus SUV that everyone knew he could not afford.

"I believe that Mr. McGregor wanted to have someone take the pet home and treat him as a member of the family, as he had," responded the attorney.

The room suddenly went quiet, and no one volunteered to care for the old man's aging pet. The attorney surveyed the room multiple times until he saw a timid hand raised in the rear of the room. A small-framed woman with dark hair stood and said, "I'll take him home with me. It is the least that anyone can do. Everyone should have a home." The attorney smiled at Sarah and nodded his head.

Parker continued, "The second and last item to go over is the disposition of Mr. Macgregor's assets." The buzzing in the room rose to a fever pitch. "Mr. Macgregor, having no living relatives has directed me to distribute two million dollars to each household in the valley." The room erupted into loud gasps of *wows, aahs, oohs* and continued to build in volume about such untold wealth, now within their grasp.

"Attention, please, ladies and gentleman. I would like to have your attention," pleaded Parker before continuing. "The only stipulation is that you must all sign this agreement by noon tomorrow agreeing you will all accept the money."

"That's it? That's all we have to do?"

"Yes, that is all you have to do... but... it must be unanimous. Everyone must agree and you must sign this document before noon tomorrow. That is the stipulation of the will."

They all laughed. Who would turn down two million dollars they wondered aloud.

The room erupted again among those in attendance unable to fathom their good fortune. The room broke out into cheers and hands slapping among all of them. They were all good friends and neighbors, but soon they would also all be millionaires. What good luck! Who would have thought the old Scotsman had that much money.

Parker asked for silence. "Let me repeat, the signing of the agreement," the attorney continued, "must be completed by twelve noon tomorrow and remember it must be unanimous or the offer is rescinded. Ladies and gentlemen this concludes the reading of the will. We will reconvene here in this conference room tomorrow at 11:30 A.M. in order to sign the conveyance documents. Good day ladies and gentlemen." He rose from his seat and left the room as they continued to buzz about their sudden and surprising good fortune.

The next day promptly at 11:30 A.M., the doors to the law firm's conference room opened and the waiting crowd of soon to be millionaires, rushed inside the large room.

Mr. Parker took his customary seat at the head of the long conference table and laid out multiple pens for everyone to come forward and sign the agreement.

"Who would like to be first to sign?"

No one budged from their seats, until finally Sarah walked up the side aisle of the plush conference room, leaned over the document, picked up one of the waiting pens, signed the document and returned to her seat near the rear of the room.

"Next?"

No one moved. Finally, one man rose. "I have a question for you first," said Lerner, an accountant, who owned the large house on the corner. "My wife and I were thinking about the old man's offer of the two million dollars. We were talking last night and frankly we think we should get more money because we have the largest house in the community."

Mr. Fenster, an engineer by trade, sprang from his seat and said, "Yeah you do but we were the first to move into the development. And since we have been living here the longest; we feel we should get more money."

"My husband," the young petite Mrs. York challenged, "is unemployed, and we are real short of cash right now, and that money would certainly help. We should get more money."

Parker, ever the attorney, not believing his eyes or his ears, watched as the group descended into a rabble. They continued to argue over why they each should get more of the old man's money, his gift to them. The ranting, arguing, and justifications went on and on, everyone having a reason of why they should get more money. Two million dollars each was just not enough for them.

The clock was ticking, and it was now five minutes before twelve, as Mr. Parker took center stage at the table and announced, "Ladies and gentlemen, you only have five minutes left for all of you to sign this document. If all of you do not sign it by noon, the offer, according to the provisions of the Will, will be rescinded. It is gone. *Finito*. I ask you all to please sign the document… now!"

They looked at one another. One of the older men, a retiree, made a move towards the table to sign the agreement. Then Mr. Scalia, the used car salesman, stood up and addressed the assembled crowd, "Listen up everyone, if you want my signature on the document, in order to make it unanimous, you will all have to agree to pay me $100,000 *each* for my signature." He pulled out an agreement from his plaid sport coat and asked everyone to sign.

The arguing, booing and yelling renewed again, this time it was louder and more heated.

Minutes later, a loud buzzer went off and silenced the crowd. It was too late. They had not signed the paper and the money was gone. Their greed had gotten the better of them.

"Ladies and gentleman the offer is no longer on the table," Parker said as he tore up the unsigned agreement. "However, in this envelope, the Macgregor Will has an addendum called a second provision in it. This was only to be opened should you not be able to unanimously agree to this transfer. The Will calls for this second envelope to be opened at this point." He opened the manila envelope and pulled out its contents, a single sheet of folded blue paper. The attorney unfolded it and read from the legal document.

"This is an addendum to my last Will and Testament:

Should there be no unanimity in agreeing to my generous $2,000,000 individual bequest to the residents of my valley, I then decree that offer is null and void and this document supersedes the prior document. It is further decreed that the individual who agreed to take my pet as a family member into their home is my rightful heir and is entitled to my entire legacy. That person shall receive all of my money, my house, and all the surrounding land to do with as they see fit. That is my wish. Good luck to all. Your humble servant, Fergus Tucker Macgregor."

They were in shock and began arguing with each other and pointing fingers at who was the cause of their misfortune. The disagreements and fighting continued even as the neighbors returned to the valley, each blaming one another for their loss of good fortune until they all left angrily to go to their individual homes. The late-night pool parties, the wild motorboat racing, and the tiki-drinking marathons, all seemed to stop within days. Quiet had returned to the valley that Fergus and Eileen had treasured so much. One by one the neighbors moved from the valley to be replaced by quieter and more subdued families intent on enjoying the beauty and tranquility of the Cairnwell Valley.

Sarah Anderson, the dark-haired resident of the guest house, cared for the aging Scottish terrier and moved into her new home, the Macgregor homestead, and found it to be very, very comfortable.

Sitting on the swing of the large front porch of the old Scottish house, gently rocking back and forth, Sarah stroked the back of the neck of her Cheshire cat, while the aging terrier Scottie, lay sleeping soundly next to her. He slept in the wonderful sunshine of the beautiful summer day.

Sarah was building another new, larger Macgregor Cottage for women, placing it next to the original one where Sarah had once lived safe and warm. The workers waved goodbye for the day, saying, "See you tomorrow, Ms. Anderson," before speeding home to their families.

Sarah sat and looked over the valley as she surveyed the acres and acres of lemon trees she had planted as a tribute to the Macgregors. It was the largest lemon grove in the state, much to the chagrin of the remaining feuding neighbors on the lake and the lemon trees now blocked the ugly view of the homes on the lake.

Sarah sat and watched a beautiful sunset every evening, as the dipping sun reflected off the lake, without the distraction of the homes below. This was the peace that the Macgregors had seen and loved. Sarah loved the tranquility of the new Cairnwell Valley. She could smell the sweet scent of the lemon blossoms and embraced it as a memory of the Macgregor's. Sitting on the swing of the wide porch, she smiled, sipping a glass of her homemade *Limoncello,* thinking of the old Scotsman. She thought that the old man would laugh at the irony of the way things turned out but she sensed he knew what would happen all along. He had accomplished what he set out to do.

# Turnin' 30

"So Ashley, tell me, what would you like for your birthday tomorrow, now that you're turnin' the big Three-0"? asked Tyler, her boyfriend of six years. He continued without waiting for an answer. "I don't even know why we are looking at the menu. We get the same thing every time we come here. Well, Ash?"

"What would you like, Tyler?"

"Our usual, two beers, a large pepperoni pizza, with anchovies on one side and French fries, topped with gravy. How's that?"

"No, I mean what do you want to do?"

"Well, we can come back here later after the movie and order the Big Kahuna Pizza and then go back to your place, if you know what I mean? What about you?"

"I want to get married."

"What?"

"I said I want to get married, not tomorrow, but before my next birthday. I want to get married. I want to have a family."

"What do you mean? What's wrong with the way things are?"

"Ty, I love you but I have a plan, I've always had a plan. I want to finish my masters, continue to teach and then settle down in a nice house, and have a family."

He gave her a blank stare.

She continued, "You know that we are doing the same things now that we did eight years ago when we met in college. I want something more, I am ready for more. Aren't you?"

"Wow, this sounds like the 'Let's get serious speech again'."

"Let's do something. All you do is sit around your apartment with the same guys that you have known since school, Mike, Leo, Rollie, Chuck, Jerry, and Raptor—and what kind of name is Raptor anyway?"

"He is trying to develop video games for sale to companies, and Raptor is his Internet name. He is way cool."

"And how many jobs have you had in the past year? You keep moving from job to job every three to four months. Some full time and some part time. The only job you seem to be able to keep is your part-time job at the golf driving range, and we both know that's just so you can get free golf balls on the range anytime you want."

"Ashley, let me explain. You know I've been working on developing a new killer app for smart phones. It'll make us a lot of dough. I keep looking for something that I enjoy doing. You wouldn't want me to stay at a job I hate now would you? Would you, Ash?"

She paused looking at him, agreeing "No, I guess not."

"I'll find something, just have patience, Ash. I have…"

"What can I get for you two lovebirds? The usual? Pizza?"

"Hi Mary. You know the drill, two beers, a large pepperoni pizza and French fries with some gravy smeared over the top. Okay?"

"You got it, kids."

"Wait, Mary, I'm going to change my order. Give me a salad with raspberry vinaigrette dressing and a glass of ice water with a slice of lemon."

"Ash, we can afford two beers for Christ's sake."

"I know we can Ty, I just don't feel like having any alcohol, you know what I mean?"

"Well okay, I guess. Is this a new phase?"

"Tyler maybe it's time to stop hangin' out with the guys and grow up a little bit. You know I turn thirty tomorrow, the big three O and I am not getting any younger. Do you plan to hang out with these guys your whole life?"

"No… not my whole life but hey let's face it Ash we have the best of both worlds, we work, we can travel, we can do whatever we want. We never have to grow up."

"Yeah, but we don't do any of that at all." She returned his blank stare. "Ty, even some of your buddies are starting to move on with their lives, like Billy."

"I know, Billy got a job in L.A. and is doing great."

"Yeah, well Billy got the same job, paying the same money that my kid brother got last month right out of college, but Billy is ten years older. Companies will look at Billy in the future and wonder how to motivate someone who dropped out for ten years and hung around video games and bars his whole life."

"Ash get real, Billy never really had his act together, come on we both know that."

"Well, he has a full-time job and is starting to get on with his life, and that's something that you don't seem to understand."

"What's that?"

"He's starting a career! I also just heard that he and Carly got engaged."

"Well, we are engaged, aren't we, Ash?"

"Tyler… I've been wearing your high school graduation ring for the last four years as an engagement ring, hoping you would replace it with a proper ring. I guess that's too much to hope for."

"Ash, that ring has a lot of sentimental value to me, come on now."

"Here's you pizza, beer, and fries. Ashley darling, your salad will be coming right out in just a minute."

"Thanks, Mary."

"Wait here it comes. Ashley darlin' did you do something different to your hair? You look different; you have a glow about you. Must be love, huh?"

"Yeah Mary, it must be love."

"Come on, Ash, let's not fight. Let's eat. I hate it when we fight about anything but especially about jobs. Oh, by the way, can you drive me by the liquor store, and I want to pick up some beer for the party tonight."

"Party?"

"Oh, Rory got a job with the government, and they are throwing him a party later. Just a bunch of the guys, you know. I thought it would be fun just to drop by for an hour or so and celebrate with the guys, drink some beer, play some video games. Okay?"

"Sure, Tyler."

"I'll be right back; I'm going to the men's room. Don't go away." He meandered back to the men's room and came back some fifteen minutes later having been sidetracked by some nearby video games.

"Hi Mary, I just went to the bathroom and came back, and Ashley's not here. Have you seen her? Is she in the ladies room?"

"She left Tyler… she told me to give you this." The waitress held out his high school ring in the palm of her hand.

"Did she say anything?"

"Yes… she said to say goodbye."

Tyler stood in disbelief.

"Oh and that'll be $26.50 for the pizza and fries."

*I don't have any money. God how am I going to pay for all of this food, and how am I going to get home or to the party?*

He reached for his cell phone. "Hello, Carol. What's up? It's Tyler. Wanna go to a party tonight?"

# Danny Dark

"Come on, Evan. It's way past your bedtime."

"Aw, come on, Aunt Sarah, can't I stay up just a while longer?" At age ten, he was the man of the house since his father never came home from the war. Now it was just his aunt Sarah, him, and his mom and after working at her job, she went off to night school.

"I want to stay up real late. All night!"

"Well, I promised your mother I would have you in bed on time, and it is already late." She looked at him, his head drooped. "Why don't you want to go to bed?"

He hesitated, then looked down before saying just above a whisper, "I'm afraid of the dark, that's why."

"I'll keep you company until you fall asleep."

"That won't help. Mom used to do that, and it didn't help me fall asleep."

"Then how about I tell you a story?"

"What story?" he asked her his eyes now wide open in anticipation.

She stuttered and stammered before saying, "Ah… my favorite, the story of Danny Dark."

He was up in a flash getting ready for bed. He loved his Aunt Sarah's stories.

Sarah had left her hometown to attend college in Boston. She finished her master's degree then landed a job teaching English at a private secondary school in New York. She had loved it in the city and only recently returned to the tiny, picturesque town of Woodstock, Vermont, after her life fell apart in the big city. It was a town still lost in the nineteen-fifties, with its white picket fences, broad green lawns, and wonderful ice cream parlors on Main Street. It was like Mayberry, frozen in time, where everyone waved to one another across the square and everyone knew your name—and your business.

"I'm ready," Evan hollered from his bedroom.

Sarah had moved into the former sewing room in her sister's small three-bedroom house and made it her new home.

"Did you brush your teeth?"

"Yes."

She entered the room and sat on a nearby chair, turning off the main light.

"Aunt Sarah, it's dark in here."

"It's okay because I'm here now, and Danny Dark will also be here."

"Who is Danny Dark?"

"I'm glad you asked. Let me tell you the story of Danny Dark. He and his mom and dad are from here. He was about your age, tall, strong, and adventuresome. Many years ago, they left for the summer to go sailing the big blue seas. They loved sailing and when they sailed from the Atlantic towards the Caribbean Sea a mighty storm came up in the Sargasso Sea." His eyes were transfixed on her, as she told him the story.

"The storm tossed the ship from left and right for hours and hours until it they were shipwrecked onto the beach of Skull Island in the Sargasso Sea. The radio was broken, and the boat was in ruins with a large a crack in the hull. As they walked the beach, happy to be alive they saw a sign stuck in the sand in a pile of skulls that read:

**All your ships / Have left their moorings /
Cast adrift / On the Sargasso Sea / Waiting for the wind /
To set your sails free to leave Skull Island.**

"His father set about the long task of repairing the boat. Danny fished and hunted for the family and brought food for their mother to prepare dinner on an open fire. Each day he hunted further from the encampment when one day he climbed a hill and found the entrance to an old cave." Young Evan leaned in close so as not to miss a word of the story.

"He wrapped some old rags he found nearby and lit them as he ventured inside. The cave was filled with spiders and mice scurrying about the floor. Just inside the dark cave, he found a skeleton leaning on an old chest, but Danny Dark wasn't afraid. He lifted the lid of the treasure chest as his flame began to fade and inside he found it filled to the top with jewels and shiny gold coins and silver bars. It had to be worth millions. He ran to get his father."

"It took them four days to carry all of the gold, silver, and jewels from the cave to the now repaired boat. They left on the next high tide and headed to their home port of Boston. As they neared the coastline, the boat began to take on water because of the heavy weight of the gold pressing the newly repaired hull. It gave way and the boat sank within miles of shore.

"They were brought home to Woodstock and buried here in their home town but… they never found Danny's body. Legend has it that his fun loving and freewheeling spirit has been seen helping people and protecting them right here in Woodstock. It has also been said that he looks after young men his same age and protects them from harm. Right at this moment he is probably in that darkened corner looking out for you to make sure that no harm ever comes to you in the dark. So you never have to be afraid of the dark anymore."

"What a great story, Aunt Sarah. You're the best."

That became their routine every night. When he climbed into bed, she told him a story of the exploits of Danny Dark. When he needed help in school, Danny Dark came to his rescue. When someone bullied him at school, Danny Dark outsmarted the bullies. When he needed the nerve to talk to a girl at the ice cream parlor, Danny Dark was there to help him.

One night she was retelling him the original story about Danny Dark and how he came back to Woodstock when Evan sat up in bed and said, "Auntie Sarah you said it wrong, Danny Dark went sailing from Boston and got shipwrecked on Skull Island."

"Right, you are absolutely correct Evan. What was I thinking?" After that she began to write down the stories she told him.

On a lark one day, she posted one of the stories on her blog—Sarah's Day in Woodstock and the number of readers at her blog tripled. People loved her stories so she continued to post them until one of her early and most loyal followers suggested she publish them in a book or an eBook.

Two months later, she did just that, and they began to sell. Then she self-published them in paperback book form, and sales took off. Her stories made Danny stronger and made her happy.

A few weeks later, she took her usual post on the chair in her nephew's room and began to tell him a Danny Dark story about being scared of the dark.

Evan interrupted her, "Aunt Sarah I'm not scared of the dark anymore now that I have Danny Dark to protect me. Can you tell me a different story?"

Flustered but proud she said, "Yes, of course Evan."

When she was leaving his room he whispered, "You can close the door, Aunt Sarah. I'm okay; I have Danny Dark with me."

"Good night, Evan. I love you."

"Good night, Auntie Sarah, I love you too."

She walked down the hallway to her room, closed the door, and began to blog on her computer about the story she had told him that night.

Evan turned over in bed and whispered, "Good night, Danny."

From the shadowy corners of the room a watchful voice responded, "Good night, Evan."

# INDIE—A Female Vigilante

(an excerpt)

Javed Khan paused and raised his hand, halting the convoy behind him. The two hunters and the gun bearers at the rear stopped, frozen in their tracks. He sniffed the air before kneeling down to examine the deep footprints in the sandy mud. The experienced tracker stood taller than the group behind him, even taller than the big American. Javed was blessed with strong hands and broad shoulders from years of working in the forests with the teak lumbermen and the elephants they used to haul the heavy loads from the jungle. The toiling in the woods had made his body and muscles hard like tempered steel.

"This is the one," he whispered, tracing the huge footprint with his finger motioning for the gun bearers to bring their weapons. "This is the one we want. He is a big one… about four meters…"

"In English please," said his annoyed American companion.

"He's ten feet tall and easily five tons. And he's close, very close."

"You can't tell all of that from a footprint!" jeered the balding American congressman from Wyoming.

"Quiet…Let me show you something." The seasoned tracker took the American newcomer's hand and retraced the outline of the big elephant footprint they had been tracking for the last three days.

"See how deep the impression is here in the dirt? That takes a mighty big animal to make such a track. Notice the bit of blood on the side of the footprint? It is probably from a poacher who tried to bring him down and failed. So he's wounded and crazed—crazy like a fox. Now squeeze the dung heap."

"What? I'm not doing that."

Javed grabbed the Congressman's arm and pushed both of their hands deep inside the steaming pile. "See? It's still warm, so he's close, real close." He stood without brushing himself off while his intense gaze scouted the tall grasses that surrounded them. "Now let's just hope it's a male. There's no way in hell I want to tangle with a female rogue Indian elephant. No, sir. They're the worst."

They walked down the path waiting for the onslaught that was sure to come. "Why do you carry that relic?" asked the nervous Yank in a hushed cautious tone pointing to his guide's .465 Holland &Holland Magnum hunting rifle.

Javed did not like to talk while he stalked his prey, especially when it was dangerous quarry like elephants. He fondly recalled hunting countless times with his father in this same rugged terrain for wild boar, rhino, water buffalo, gaur, bears and tigers. Now his childhood hunting instincts returned to him. His American companion carried the special government permit, which allowed them to track the crazed elephant that had been terrorizing his family's ancestral homestead. He came home to hunt this rogue and put an end to the panic in the village he grew up in as a child.

"Why? Because it works, that's why," Javed replied dryly.

"I'll stick with my .460 Weatherby Magnum," boasted the Yank. "This high velocity baby will bring down a Sherman tank."

"Or go right through him… and not stop him at all. If it doesn't hit his brain at the back of his skull then he'll keep charging you."

The seasoned tracker realized how much he missed being out in the bush, and he was happy to see his mother again during this visit. They shared a meal in the same small one-room house where he was born and grew up in.

His mother had prepared a simple lunch for him before he left for the hunt—fritters in yogurt, beans. She had baked his favorite, a puffy bread called *puri*, accompanied by her traditional homemade tea. He loved her tea, which she made by boiling the tea leaves in a mix of water, milk and spices, such as cardamom, cloves, cinnamon and ginger. His mouth still resonated from the taste of his favorite childhood meal. One day he would come back here, he vowed to himself, back to his birthright. He could always make a living here as a guide he reasoned.

The Yank pestered him again as he scouted to the left and to the right for their quarry. "What do you do in the real world when you're not hunting rogue elephants in the wilds of India?" asked the nervous American now clinging close to his Indian guide.

"I've been a police detective in New Delhi for the last twelve years."

"Homicide?"

"No, I was in homicide until last year. Now I'm assigned to the Metro Transit Division."

"Yeah, who did you piss off to get that job?"

They were careful not to step and break any branches that would make a loud sudden noise. The jungle had grown quiet.

"The governor." His ears perked up at a slight movement in front of them. "Quiet… Shhhh…" He raised four fingers on his left hand high in the air signaling eighty yards, off to the left. Javed slid the powerful rifle from his shoulder and quietly released the safety. The beast was close. He could almost feel the breath of the mighty animal beat on his face. The caravan stopped. His hunting companion beside him held his rifle in the ready position. Then all at once, their world changed.

They felt the ground quake before they saw the massive beast charge them. The elephant trumpeted its arrival with its head raging from side to side, the large flailing ears, its raw eyes signaled its only desire— stomp them dead into the earth. Five tons of anger charged them in a split-second. Eighty yards and closing fast.

Javed readied his rifle. Sixty yards.

"This one's mine," said the Yank, raising his rifle to his shoulder. The squatty hunter closed his left eye while he sighted the rogue elephant over the long barrel of his weapon. He squeezed off a roaring round of death headed straight for the huge bull elephant. Fifty yards. It kept coming. Forty yards. Charging. He pulled the trigger a second time. Again the air was filled with the blast of gunpowder, and again it failed to stop the charging beast. His rifle was empty. He fumbled to reload, dropping the shells onto the grassy green earth. Thirty yards. The branches on the trees shook violently announcing the unwelcome arrival of the huge angry animal.

The monstrous trumpet of the elephant blared then roared, its head held high in rage. The sound was deafening like that of a roaring avalanche. The ground shook beneath them. It was a storm of terror headed straight for them.

They could see its wild eyes.

It lowered its head to charge for the kill. Twenty yards.

Javed raised his rifle to his shoulder then steadied his weapon. His hand was firm as he squeezed the trigger. Ten yards. The weapon belched fire from the muzzle and propelled the killing shot through the elephant's forehead. The beast dropped dead to the ground in a crash of rage landing mere feet from where they stood. The earth shook, and dust rose high above them in huge clouds from the tremendous weight of its fall. There was no sign of life left from the once-powerful animal.

The mighty King of India lay humbled and dead before them. Javed walked to the side of the magnificent beast.

His terrified foreign companion stood frozen with fear. A large wet area of moisture ringed the front of his khaki bush pants. "Good shot," he finally managed in a hollow whisper to Javed. "I must... get me one of those guns."

Javed walked around the magnificent dead creature and examined him, more as an anthropologist than as a hunter examining his kill. A trail of blood streamed down the side of the silent brute. He traced it to a festering wound made by the tip of a spear, which still dangled from its side. Just what he anticipated, a poacher. He stroked the surface of the once-proud animal and stood to say his farewells and pay his final respects. He had reverence for all creatures, but this mighty beast was one closest to his heart, and he was glad it was over.

Javed's job was done, and it was time for him to return to New Delhi. While he loved being home, he missed the sights and sounds and excitement of the city. He missed the late-night dinners and enjoyed the tastes and captivating aromas of all the different foods he grew up with.

He missed the pulsating excitement of the capital. While he loved the intoxicating thrill of the bush country, he was always torn as to where his home truly was in India. Anytime he was away from the city he missed the noise and the massive crush of people and the telling allure of the women of New Delhi, some of the most beautiful women on earth. But most of all he missed his Tasha, his spunky fourteen-year-old daughter. She was his precious pearl. This coming weekend was his time with her. He was going to make the most of their weekend before he returned her to her mother's house Sunday night but for now, it was time to pack up and head home. Yes, he must admit, Delhi was now home for him, and he hurried to get back. Now all he had to do...

*Read more of the novel INDIE –available wherever fine books are sold-*

# Diana Margarita

I love Nicholas Sparks. I always have and always will. I love his writing, his stories, his descriptions, his way with words, and his way with women. I love this writer because he makes me cry—usually you hate somebody who makes you cry, but Nicholas Sparks draws tears from my eyes and I love it.

My hotheaded Peruvian lover of a husband, Tonio, knows of my secret love for this man. How he could not know with Sparky's (my nickname for Nicholas Sparks) books filling our bookshelves, scattered about the floor throughout our small bungalow, and sprinkled throughout my SUV? The DVDs from all of his movies are stacked high above the television. My Kindle has every one of his eBooks so I can read them on the go, sitting at a traffic light or waiting in line at the grocery store. As I said, I love Nicholas Sparks and love to read his books.

My name is Diana Margarita. I am twenty-nine years old, and teach Spanish to underprivileged kids in a school outside of Washington D.C. I have a beautiful four-year-old son who we named Nicholas, and he is the image of his father.

My husband is in the diplomatic service and travels a lot. During the summer, I work for my father as a Workers Compensation Private Investigator at his insurance agency. I think he does this to keep an eye on me and to help my family with finances.

My first assignment for my father was to track down two unemployed men who were abusing Workers Compensation Disability Insurance. My friend Star and I looked for them for hours at the address my father gave me. No luck so we finally gave up our search. I pulled out my Nicholas Sparks book as we stopped for lunch at a barrio sandwich truck and noticed a hunk of a man with his shirt off lifting pieces of engine blocks while showing off for some friends... and us. They saw us and smiled. Too bad I was married. He was joined by another man and they took turns lifting these heavy blocks of metal.

My friend Star and I took pictures of them with our cell phones and sent them to our friends. Unfortunately one was sent to my father. He texted me back, "Great job these are the two we have been trying to catch." Sometimes you just get lucky. Go figure.

I suspect I am deeply neurotic, anal-compulsive, slightly paranoid, claustrophobic, subject to motion sickness, given to fits of panic attacks, and a member of Mensa. I love to go to the Mensa meetings with my friend Star (her real name is Stephanie Arnold, but she took to being called Star, once she was accepted by Mensa, the so-called genius society.)

When I went for my test at the downtown Mensa office the damn receptionist was reading *The Flowers of Evil* by Baudelaire, and had a pile of books on her desk written by Jean Paul Sartre, Albert Camus, Ayn Rand, and Jacques Derrida. She asked me if I wanted to read anything while I waited, pointing to her stack of nearby books. I told her 'no thank you,' I brought my own and pulled my worn copy of *The Notebook* by my old friend Nicholas Sparks from my handbag, and began to read.

The admissions test was dumb, and I was finished before the rest of the small-assembled group was halfway through. They sent me a letter welcoming me into the group stating that I had scored a 166, a near record for their region. I found out later that Star was the current local record holder at 171.

We made quite a pair walking into our first Mensa meeting. Star was dressed in all black, with black lipstick, torn black mesh nylons, black nail polish, and enough body piercings to set off the metal detector. She even had a dragon tattoo done on her ankle.

I, in contrast, wore my tight jeans, cowboy boots, push up bra, and walked into the meeting with my blonde hair falling just so over my shoulders. I looked great if I do say so myself.

We didn't last too long that night before they asked us for our membership card and said they wanted to review their admissions policy. Fat chance of us ever getting back in again, I guess.

A week or so later I was so excited when I saw an ad in the local newspaper for a summer writing class at the local community college. I joined immediately. The class was titled "Write like Nicholas Sparks in Six Weeks." The class consisted of a group of women of assorted ages, and one man. The teacher walked around the room and asked everyone who was their favorite author. I promptly raised my hand and said, "Nicholas Sparks of course."

The older woman next to me said "Nora Roberts."

"Why Nora Roberts?" asked the instructor.

The old woman paused for a moment before she added, "I love Nora Roberts—her stories and the way she tells them."

The teenager next to her said, "I also love Nora Roberts for the same reason."

"Nora Roberts? Humph." The sole male member of our group mumbled under his breath. "James Patterson, now there's a writer." Everyone looked at him strangely.

Twin sisters both chimed in, "Janet Evanovich, Janet Evanovich" at the same time.

The brooding man whispered again, "James Patterson."

A woman in the long yellow dress, raised her hand and said, "*Fifty Shades of Grey.*"

The tall raven-haired instructor leaned close to her and whispered, "Yes, dear, but whom is your favorite author?"

"Oh… Fifty Shades of Grey. "

"Then E.L. James is your favorite author?"

"E.L. James? Oh yes, *Fifty Shades of Grey* and oh yes, I love H.M. Ward. H.M. Ward writes the best books ever. I love H.M. Ward."

Exasperated, she moved on to the man in flannel shirt with an unwrapped cigar sticking from his pocket. "And you, sir?"

"Oh my favorite writer would have to be…James Patterson."

She turned to the group watching her and said, "Well class, your assignment for next week is to read the book *A Message in a Bottle* by Nicholas Sparks and be prepared to discuss it next week. I would like to have all of you write a report about what you would change if you were writing the book. Have a great time."

During the week, I started to write the report many times, but all I could think about was my Tonio. He was coming home tomorrow. I had not seen him or been with him for four weeks.

My darling Antonio was coming home so Nicholas, Star, and I went shopping to prepare a special homecoming for him. We stopped at the local department store and bought some clothes and lingerie, things I knew he would love. The Perfect Shoe was our next stop. It's a specialty shoe boutique, my favorite. Star and I love that store.

A new salesclerk at the checkout counter looked up from the book he was reading to greet us. "Good morning, ladies. Can I point you in the right direction?"

He was new, very new if he didn't know who we were. We were the store's best customers. We had shopped at this store twice a week for years. You see my other secret passion is shoes… boots… sandals, slippers, or anything else I can put on my feet. I love shoes. Antonio converted our spare bedroom into a closet to house all of my shoes. Star and I went to the checkout counter to pay for the shoes we selected. He loaded my purchases into a large shopping bag and thanked me.

He was ringing Star's purchases when she noticed the book he was reading, *The Brothers Karamazov* by Dostoyevsky. "Good book?" she asked him as he rang up the shoes.

He looked at her then resumed his sales activity. "Yes. I'm in an advanced honors class at the university, and this is one of the more difficult ones to understand."

"You're cute. Has anyone ever told you that before?"

He squirmed and had to start again. "No …but thank you."

She picked up the book and began casually flipping through it. "You're right. Not that easy to read, but I like the ending."

"Yeah, sure."

"No, I enjoyed it."

He stopped doing what he was doing and turned to face her. "Are you trying to tell me that you read that book in the twenty seconds you breezed through it just now?"

"Yeah."

"Bullshit."

"No, I did."

"Bullshit."

"Tell you what. I have a photographic memory coupled with the ability to speed read anything, and I never forget anything I read. I bet you I can answer any question you can ask of me regarding this book."

"How much?" asked the young clerk of the woman standing in front of him.

She looked at the shoes piled high on the counter. "If I answer your question I get the shoes free."

"And if you don't?" he asked looking at her wearing her snug jeans and tight low-cut top.

"If I don't, then… I'll…" she leaned closer and whispered in his ear. His face broadened with the glow of a huge smile.

"Yes? You would do that?"

"A bet is a bet. Ask your question."

He picked up the book and thumbed through it, looking for some obscure question to stump her on. Then he stopped. He had his question. "How much money did Fyodor Pavlovich promise to give Grushenka if she becomes his lover?" He smiled.

She pouted then struck a pose. "Wow… that's some question."

"Ahh!"

"He promised to give her three thousand rubles."

His smile faded away.

She kissed him on the cheek and whispered something in his ear as she grabbed her bag of shoes.

"How did you know the answer to his question? I know your reading ability is off the charts but this… that was incredible. How did you do it?"

Star smiled, "I just finished reading the book over the weekend for the third time. That was a piece of cake."

I laughed. "What did you say to him as we left the store?"

"I thought he was cute. I told him I would be back at closing time, and we could hang out later." We both laughed.

The next day I would drop little Nicholas off to spend the night with my mom and dad who adored him. I could then concentrate on getting "reacquainted" with my Latin lover of a husband.

When I was finishing my report for my writing class I thought of nothing but him. *Damn him*, four weeks was much too long for him to leave me here alone. Yes, the only company I had when he was away was books, my music and… my Nicholas Sparks. I only had to wait one more day. Just one more day…

Late that night the phone rang. I didn't recognize the name on the caller ID. "Hello?" I whispered, always afraid of late-night phone calls.

"Mrs. Margarita? Mrs. Antonio Margarita? This is Nicholas. I need to talk to you about…"

# A Second Chance

(An excerpt)

Ravenna Morgan removed her robe and entered the quiet pool—naked—wearing only the thin gold chain and the dangling, gold Celtic cross, she had worn since she was young. She swam with ease in the hotel's private lap pool, enjoying her daily, early morning swim.

Water glided over her body as she dipped her hands in front of her, crossing the pool with measured, elegant strokes. Her long red hair floated behind her. The soothing water massaged her athletic body and caressed her curves as she left gentle ripples in her wake.

She knew she could swim here, just outside her modest apartment, and not be disturbed. It was one of the few benefits she truly enjoyed as the on-site resident manager of the Hotel Petros.

There was another pool for guests in the front of the hotel. From there, you could see for miles past the turquoise blue waters of the Aegean Sea. While it featured the most spectacular, panoramic views of the island and the waters beyond, her pool featured tree-shrouded seclusion. She treasured her privacy.

The hotel was empty, which was common at this time of the season. The large, private luxury yachts would come at the end of the month, and their passengers stayed to enjoy the beautiful beaches and her fabulous cooking. They would be making their southern sojourn before heading north, back to the more populated islands, like Mykonos. Here, they were far from all of the other islands, and she liked it that way.

When they came, the wealthy men would drool over the tall, shapely Irish beauty, and even her gold wedding band did not stop them from making their usual advances. Sometimes it would take the presence of her better half, Trevor, to cool the hot passion of some of her more amorous visitors.

But by and large, most guests were gracious and appreciated the laid-back atmosphere and lifestyle on the beautiful island of Petros. They came to enjoy the splendor of the crystal blue water for swimming and diving, along with the fine sandy beaches on the other side of the island. But most of them only wanted a long hot shower, a good meal, a full-sized bed, and the opportunity to listen to Ravenna strum her guitar and sing around the patio fireplace at night. Even life aboard a luxury yacht becomes tedious after a while.

On the tiny island, there was no television, no cell phone service, no radio signals, and spotty Internet service. But the hotel offered plenty of peace and quiet high atop the hill, and it was the quiet, laid back atmosphere that Ravenna had come to love.

Her regular visitors, after they left the island, would send her music and books. She loved cookbooks and travel books. The hotel had stacks of CDs sitting at the front desk outside the bar, sent from her guests as they made their journeys around the globe. She loved to listen to the music and she loved to dance. The one thing she did miss was the dancing more than anything else. Trevor no longer liked to dance. "Too tiring," he would always say.

When she finished her swim and toweled off, she showered, then dressed for a day in town. She pulled on her loose-fitting Levi's cutoffs, slipped on her handmade leather sandals, and tossed on an old Greek peasant blouse, cut low to reveal her ample female charms.

The tall, striking beauty, with her emerald green eyes, youthful figure, and morning glory smile, felt right at home on this slow-paced island paradise. At age forty-four, she could have easily passed for someone ten years younger. She was easy to pick out in a crowd and stood in stark contrast to the dark-haired, older island women who usually dressed in black. Her beauty even rivaled the younger female residents who, with their flashing eyes, dark hair, and mysterious good looks, were some of the most beautiful women on earth.

She reread Trevor's note, which he had left on her bedside table for her to find when she awoke that morning.

R—<br>
I did not want to wake you.<br>
Will be back in a week.<br>
See you soon.<br>
Trevor

Trevor and Michel, the hotel's occasional fix-it man, had already left for the ferry. She hated to see Trevor go, even though it was only for a week. She had said her goodbyes the night before because she detested long farewells at the ferry. Dressed, she headed for the lobby of the small hotel.

She positioned the welcome sign on the registration counter. It directed those who found their way to the hotel to sign in, choose a room key, and make themselves at home. Everything was very informal and relaxed at her island hotel hideaway. Hotel Petros was one of two hotels. The other hotel on the island was Zorbas, which catered to Greek visitors from the other side of the island and wayward ferryboat passengers who got off on the wrong island.

Ravenna grabbed a flower from a pink trailing vine near the hotel's deep blue swinging entrance gates. She pinned the blossom behind her ear and took in a deep breath of fresh air.

She was always in awe of the view from her hilltop hotel. Far in the distance, she could see the nearest islands, over an hour away by fishing boat. She noticed the bustling village below and the shallow, light blue water that surrounded the island. From her hillside perch, she gazed further out at the calming, azure Aegean Sea, the blue shades becoming darker as the water became deeper. It was a breathtaking sight. Down below was the harbor town of Thios.

As Ravenna made her way down the steep hill into town for her grocery shopping, she sang to keep her mind off Trevor's departure. The pretty Irish American lass hummed an old Irish tune, "*Carrickfergus.*" She loved the ancient Irish song she had learned as a child from her parents. She was born in western Ireland, outside of the small town of Limerick, but moved with her family to St. Louis when her father got a job with an American company.

The road down to the village of Thios was partially paved with irregular, peanut-sized rocks. The loose stones kicked out from under her sandals, sending them bouncing in front of her. She watched them roll down the dusty road.

She passed row upon row of brightly colored flowers, hanging from vines everywhere. Their colors harmonized with the colors of the rainbow. She sniffed the blooms of her favorite flowers, including the lemon yellow claritis, dark purple bougainvilleas, and the magnificent hot pink passionflowers.

While some flowers clung to nearby fences, others sprouted from old stone pots and anywhere else these beautiful wild flowers could find an inch of earthly ground. Flowers staked their claim to the overgrown telephone poles and dangled from telephone wires. Ironic, she thought, that the phone lines were good for something, since it was next to impossible to make calls off the island. She loved the flowers and the sweet fragrances that always filled the air around her home.

Ravenna glanced at the beautiful vista and thought about how much she loved it there. She smiled. Maybe today would be a good day after all. Her thoughts drifted back to her childhood in St. Louis and the many friends she'd left behind so many years ago. Her imagination filled her with wonder. *Whatever happened to them? And him?* Walking toward the village, she was lost in these ruminations. But soon her past would come rushing back to her, and quicker than she'd ever imagined.

---

"Come on, you old slow poke, get a move on," shouted Gabi Branigan to her husband Jack, as she sprinted down the side street to the beach, leading him by more than four lengths. She ran track in college and stayed in great shape all the years of their marriage.

"Okay, okay, I'll give you a race for your money," Jack responded. One of these times, he would like to outrun her. Just once. She was competitive by nature, and he was never able to beat her. Jack stretched his long frame and pumped his legs to the maximum. Glancing up, he noticed he was closing in on her.

When she turned her head, shock registered on her face; he was gaining distance. Running faster, she pulled somewhat ahead. She was not going to lose to anyone, not even her loving husband Jack.

He closed the distance and was soon neck and neck with his erstwhile opponent. One last push and then he passed her, making it to the beach four strides ahead of her. He'd beaten her! For once in his life he had beaten his wife Gabi in a footrace. He would never let her live this down.

"I know, I know you were tired and out of shape. I understand," he said to her, huffing and puffing, still out of breath.

"You don't need to make any excuses for me." She smiled, with a pout beginning to grow on her lips, looking for sympathy despite her protests to the contrary.

He pulled her close and leaned forward to kiss her. He could feel her pressing into him, her heart still racing from their chase, her breasts firm as his lips neared hers. It was so good to see her smile again. He went to hold her closer, to kiss her…

*WHOOOO!!!!* … *WHOOOO!!!!* … *WHOOOO!!!!* …

The deep baritone sound of the Greek island ferry horn boomed loud overhead, startling Jack from his sleep; in an instant, his dream dissolved, and Gabi was gone.

The sound cracked the air and broke the silence on the rusting ship. It blasted a deep hello, announcing its presence: *WHOOOO!!!!... WHOOOO!!!!... WHOOOO!!!!...*

The sound was distant, as if it did not matter to him. He was tired and glad to finally get some rest. It felt good just to lie there on the lower bunk bed of the slow-moving inter-island ferry. If he tried hard, he wondered if he could he pick up his dream where he left off—he had outraced Gabi! Probably not, he finally concluded. With half-opened eyes, he surveyed his surroundings, then remembered where he was—a small cabin onboard an old Greek ferry on his way to the island of Mykonos.

A cute, young booking agent in the port of Piraeus persuaded him to upgrade to a "cabin suite" on the ferry. He was so tired he would have agreed to anything that the pretty young thing talked him into buying. She smiled at him the entire time as he completed the necessary paperwork. She had probably made a nice commission on the upgrade he thought.

As it was, he just barely fit in his "upgraded" bunk bed. It was obviously made for much shorter passengers. Jack was different from the typical men on the ferryboat. He was tall, with broad shoulders, unruly sandy-colored hair, and deep blue eyes, he sported an easy smile and was devilishly handsome. Although he wasn't aware of how good-looking he was, women seated near him in restaurants always strained to watch him walk past, much to Gabi's chagrin.

He did not relish spending any more time in the overcrowded city of Athens since the strike had immobilized the city, filling every hotel room with stranded travelers. In the narrow roads of the capital, taxis jammed the streets, bringing traffic to a standstill. In the hot, late-June sun, every restaurant had lines of patrons outside waiting to be seated.

Even though he hated traveling by ship, he decided it was worth the trouble to get to Mykonos early rather than stay in Athens. It turned out he was wrong. Jack hated boats, and he abhorred small ones in particular, but he had no choice except to take the ferry to reach his destination—the Greek airlines strike had crippled all air travel in the country. He loathed the water; the rolling of the boat in the choppy seas made him seasick. He could not wait for the ride to be over.

Before he settled in his small cabin, he wiped every handle, doorknob, and surface he might touch with his anti-bacterial wipes which he always carried. He brushed off the mattress of the bunk bed with his hand to clear away any lingering foreign objects. His loving wife Gabi always preached to him that you could never be too careful where germs and dirt were concerned.

Snubbing out his cigarette in the dirty *Cinzano* ashtray, he vowed again he would quit smoking soon. He had brought three cartons of cigarettes with him from the States, and when those were gone, he was going to quit, again. *Promise!* Yes, he would quit, soon. Gabi always detested the rank odor of his cigarette smoke.

Jack turned his sport coat inside out and used it as a pillow to try to get some sleep. He rolled over on the short bed, dreaming of the quiet solitude of the luxury accommodations of a suite at the Prince Edward Hotel on Mykonos. He and Gabi had stayed there five years earlier and loved it. It was clean but expensive, and worth every penny. Jack smiled, thinking of the hotel. It was like staying at an upscale New York resort. The hotel was new, with hot showers and room service that served hamburgers. *Yes, that's the ticket,* he thought.

The cabin on the ferry he rented for the six-hour journey to Mykonos was not much larger than a typical American walk-in closet. It also shared many of the same smells. The air in the room was stale and clammy. He turned over on the cabin's narrow bunk bed, trying to get comfortable after his twenty-hour, three-airline journey from Chicago, before he fell back to sleep.

Soon the ship's horn sounded again and again. *WHOOOO!!!!*... *WHOOOO!!!!*... *WHOOOO!!!!*... The noise caused him to sit up in the small bed, and he struggled to look out of the tiny porthole in his cabin. He could see the deep blue Aegean Sea in the distance and the crystal clear, light-blue water near the ship. The small island town was retreating in the distance.

He looked to the hills beyond the village. As an architect, he admired the architectural simplicity of the windmills high atop the hills, functional in their design and yet graceful in action, spinning ever so slowly. Jack could feel himself already starting to relax and enjoy his two-week hiatus. He only had to endure this final boat ride to his destination. He came to Greece ten days early for the annual family reunion, so he could just relax on the beach at the Prince Edward and begin writing his book. He would enjoy the peace and quiet of the islands.

His normal travel schedule was horrendous; he traveled the globe non-stop as the front man for his international design firm. After the family reunion on Mykonos, he hoped things would settle down. Then he was off to a two-month assignment in Australia for his company.

Jack would travel to Australia as an architectural/engineering liaison, to consult with the U.S. and Australian governments on a project being built out in the northern desert of Australia. Even the Aussies, who were used to the rugged outback, called the building site the "boonies." Luckily he would be working in the city of Sydney in a comfortable, air-conditioned office, soaking up Australian hospitality for two months. What a life, he thought, but it was getting old. He lay back down.

The old ferry's horn boomed again, rousing him, and shaking the old boat to its sixty-year-old core. *WHOOOO!!!!* ... *WHOOOO!!!!*...

Jack froze. *Oh, my God!* Panic set in. The boat was leaving the pier—he'd overslept! *The windmills. The white buildings. The blue doors.* He was at Mykonos! This was his stop!

The inter-island ferryboat was pulling away from the dock. Jack panicked, grabbed his bags, jacket, sunglasses, cigarettes, cell phone, and his book from the small bedside table, and made a mad dash for the gangplank. He ran down the narrow passageway, already overcrowded with passengers heading to other islands.

"Mykonos?" he asked an old woman dressed in black, standing in the hallway.

"Mykonos," she responded with a toothy grin.

He ran as fast as he could manage, slipping on the floor of the old passageway, nearly tripping over a man in a wheelchair who was blocking his way.

"Sorry," he said, without pausing to look back.

"Hoy, no problem, mate," came the understanding response from the man.

*WHOOOO!!!!* The horn blared again. He could see them throwing off the ropes from ashore and the ship pulling away from the old dock. Jack would have to jump for it. He strapped one bag over his head and shoulders and threw another ashore. It landed squarely on the old wooden pier. He threw his next bag. It hit the dock, bounced off and splashed into the murky waters churned up by the propellers of the rusty old ferry. He looked down as the leather bag floated by before disappearing into the waters below. His cigarettes were in that bag. *No time to dwell on it now*, he thought.

Jack leaped to the pier, landed, and teetered on the edge, but made a safe landing.

The horn blasted a final time, saying farewell.

Jack waved goodbye and good riddance to the old ferryboat. He turned and watched it chug away to the next island, leaving the dock behind. Jack scoured the nearby waters for evidence of his drowning bag, but it was gone. *Damn.* Well, at least he'd made it. He walked down the long pier toward the town, pulling his luggage behind him. The roll-on suitcase made a *clunk, clunk, clunk* noise as the hard plastic wheels hit the spaces between the boards on the old wooden pier.

The island looked smaller than he remembered, as he clunked down the long dock. Mykonos was his wife Gabriella's favorite Greek island. That was probably why her sister, Joanie, suggested it for this year's family reunion, knowing that Jack would never object to such a choice. Well, at least it was better than last year's choice of Boise, Jack's sister-in-law Sarah's hometown. Next year was his turn, and his choice was going to be Sicily, where Gabriella's parents were born. They could stay at The Sicilian Grand Resort Hotel. He smiled to himself.

Jack could feel the warmth of the island sun on his face. The breeze off the water cooled the afternoon heat. It felt good. He and Gabi always loved the Greek islands and visited them often. But now, because of his constant traveling, he preferred the bigger islands with their newer hotels. They were clean, efficient, and had twenty-four hour room service. Made him feel more at home, plus they served those American-style hamburgers.

As he made his way to the end of the pier, a group of young boys, all in sandals and t-shirts, approached him, with dark, tanned faces, coal black hair, and brilliant white, flashing smiles.

"American? Canadian? You need bed? Place for stay? Food?" peppered the tallest one and the apparent leader of the ragtag group.

"T-shirt? You like?" interrupted the smallest one, pushing in front of the group, trying to sell his wares. He held up a t-shirt with the ubiquitous blue-and-white flag of Greece emblazoned on the front. He was soon pushed aside by the leader.

"I Stavros," he told the weary American. "My uncle, Nicolai, he own hotel downtown, Zorbas. You follow me. You like, I guarantee." The tall lad attempted to grab Jack's bag and lead him down the small main street to his uncle's hotel.

"No, thank you. I'm with a group of family members. I'm looking for the Prince Edward Hotel. Can you tell me how to find it? I have a reservation there."

"Prince Edward Hotel?" mocked the tall one named Stavros. His smile turned to a snicker.

"Yes, I'm looking for The Prince Edward," Jack repeated, suddenly weary from his long trip.

Stavros said something indiscernible in Greek to the assembled group of young friends. When he finished speaking, they all laughed and then began to point at him, laughing all the while.

"What is so funny?" Jack asked. The boys reached the end of the pier, and the group parted to allow Jack to read the blue-and-white sign, which proudly proclaimed in three languages:

WELCOME TO THE ISLAND OF PETROS

*Petros? What the hell? No! It couldn't be.* Jack had gotten off on the wrong island. Now what was he going to do? The town looked so small. They probably didn't even have hot running water here. He'd have a glass a wine in town and wait for the next ferry. It couldn't be that long of a wait.

"When is the next ferry to Mykonos?" he asked the tall one.

"No ferries for another week, my American friend. Next Friday. Welcome to Petros! Enjoy your stay. See you in town at uncle's hotel. Goodbye, see you in town."

Great, what more can happen?

*Read more of the novel A Second Chance–available wherever fine books are sold-*

# Dog with No Name

The anxious puppy bounded back and forth in the rear of the car waiting for his owners to return from their visit to the roadside store. It was early July in suburban Maryland and near evening but still hot inside even with the window slightly opened to let in some cooling air for the puppy.

They had not been gone long, but even minutes seem like an eternity for a black Lab puppy. He lay in his cushioned bed and played with his rubber bone, gnawing it intensely, before shaking it towards the rear of the SUV. He pounced on it. Looking up, his dark brown eyes narrowed when he saw a potential prey outside the window. It was a small furry brown rabbit with his white cottontail wiggling while he nibbled on the plentiful grass at the edge of the parking lot, minding his own business.

The puppy's hunting primordial instincts took over, and he stilled at the first sight of his quarry. He crouched low and crept closer to the back of the SUV. He stuck his wet snout through the window and his powerful nose could now smell his target. He could feel the adrenalin and the juices of the hunt course through his body. He had to figure a way to get out.

The rabbit hopped along the side of the big silver SUV, looking up, tempting the dog to come after him, seeming to be fully aware of the puppy's vehicular confines. The dog pawed the side of the car while following the rabbit's every move with his watchful eyes, focused now only on his prey. The rabbit stopped, picked up his head, sniffed the air to ensure he was still safe and proceeded past the last of the cars before stopping at the edge of a nearby field.

The pup could not contain himself any longer and let an out an anguished yelp and ran back and forth from the front to the rear of the car, slobbering the windows with his long wet tongue for good measure.

His heart was beating fast, he set his paws on the side of the door, when suddenly the door handle went down, and the weight from the young dog caused the door to open. With one bountiful leap, he was outside and with two more huge jumps, he was upon the rabbit before the rabbit could comprehend what was happening.

The rabbit skirted to the left, fast, then to the right to outmaneuver the gangling, inexperienced, but game puppy. The chase was on.

The rabbit had an advantage, running through the familiar high grassy field with the energetic puppy close behind him. He ran fast, making sharp unexpected turns to try to lose the inexperienced pup in the overgrown grasses and bushes but to no avail. The game puppy stayed right with him.

The oversized pup was gaining on him, snipping at his haunches, but catching only wisps of fur in his mouth. The jackrabbit ran into the stream, through a watery viaduct, out to the other side with the lab now right behind him.

The pup could make out the indentations on the rabbits paws just ahead of him. The heated chase continued with both breathing hard. Every time the Labrador thought he had the rabbit in his clutches he would slip away. But he was closing on him.

It was only a matter of time and they both knew how it would end. The puppy was only interested in the chase and not the bounty. He made one last grasp and had the rabbit in his jaws, but when he landed his footing slipped and he went tumbling down the slippery ravine, end over end, losing the rabbit in the process. He heard him scampering away through the rustling leaves leaving a telltale sound as to the departing direction of the now safe and very lucky rabbit.

The pup, out of breath and with a bruised ego, tried to regain his footing and climb out of the deep muddy gulch. The slippery leaves on the side of the hill caused him to tumble back down into the ravine. He ran further down the gully and tried again, only to achieve the same result. Finally, he created enough momentum to power himself up the hill to the crest from where he came. He was safe.

Once at the top he heard a noise, then another, his keen nose detecting a strange and unfamiliar scent. It was a dangerous smell. He heard the noise again, this time behind him. He moved forward. Looking back and forth, and then in front of him, moving slowly he crossed into a small clearing and came face to face with a large, menacing German shepherd.

He faced him and lowered his head in self-preservation while the canine slowly retracted the side of his mouth, showing his large deadly pincers, clean and gleaming from regular use. The wild dog snarled a low rumbling growl while his eyes narrowed like radar on a target.

The inexperienced lab backed up slowly, while still keeping his watchful eyes on the shepherd, careful to maintain his footing. He could not afford to fall into the ravine again and be trapped down there with this huge beast ready to pounce on him.

He was distracted by a sound to the right of him, then to the left and saw three more dogs of various breeds all eyeing him, moving slowly towards him, encircling him. He lifted his lip to show that he too had strong white teeth and was a force to be reckoned with; he would not go down without a fight.

He saw some movement to his left, and when he turned to see what it was, the waiting shepherd struck, his white razor sharp teeth going right for his throat. He missed his target but the attacker latched onto the leather collar his master had put on him. It held, and they rolled over on the ground with the other creatures of the night joining in to help their leader. The group yelped in support of their leader while others howled in anticipation of what was to come. They moved in closer for the kill.

The Lab was young but strong and spun the big shepherd around in a circle. The lab finally swung their leader into the eight dogs surrounding them as the collar snapped and he was free from the weight around his neck.

The others attacked and nipped his rear, then his legs in an effort to inflict damage and pain to the interloper. It hurt as the first blood was drawn.

The noise of the fight and the barking of the wild dogs alerted other nearby dogs to join in the fight and the growling and gnashing of wild teeth reached a mad pitch. They were out for blood, they could smell it, they could taste it, and they were not going to be denied their prize.

When he turned he found himself in the middle of a circle, facing a dozen wild, snarling and famished dogs. He was not one of them so he was fair game. Blood ran down his one eye, closing his vision.

When he turned to keep them in front, the ones behind him slashed his rear haunches, drawing blood. They attacked again and again, weakening his rear leg. He knew he had to do something. He charged the mixed-breed boxer and then immediately pulled back causing the circle around him to expand and then contract.

The two in front of him took up the charge and when they lunged towards him, he moved sideways and they landed in the ravine behind him. He saw the opening they left behind and took off running fast and hard, the angry horde of famished animals close behind him, yelping, and calling others to join in the hunt. The pack lived for the chase but he was young and strong but he was now hurt and bleeding and only able to see out of one eye. He ran for his life.

The wild dog pack was gaining on him. Running at full speed, he heard the familiar sound of automobiles and trucks on the road ahead. He made for the highway and crossed just in front of a large, horn blowing eighteen-wheeler, blasting his air horn into the now darkening night. The Lab made it across the road just in time. The truck hit the first two in the front of the pack behind him in a bloody crush of bodies. The hauler disappeared down the night highway, followed by other headlights and horns raking the night.

The leader of the mangy bunch, the snarling dark shepherd, stopped his pack and waited before turning the disappointed group back to the woods to look for other game. He turned and his dark eyes looked in the direction of where the lab had gone. *Another time,* he thought. He would wait. He would be there, waiting and when he saw him again, he would kill him.

The black Lab ran like the devil himself was chasing him and he did not stop, until he was miles away from the angry pack of canine carnivores. He sniffed the air and sniffed the ground for a scent to take him back to his family, but it was of no use. They were nowhere to be found. The pup was lost and alone.

He slept that night in a concrete drainpipe abandoned by the side of the road, licking his wounds hoping the pain would leave him. He could see in the moonlight the gashes made by the teeth of the hounds he met that night.

At dawn, he made his way through the woods, past some stores and saw a familiar sight, the family Jeep. He bounded towards it but was greeted by strangers shooing away the bloodied and wild-eyed looking dog. He had never seen fear from people before as they threw soda cans at him before retreating into their family vehicle. He licked the sweet liquid, his tongue dry and crusty. It did not help.

The puppy walked along the side of the road in what he thought was the general direction of home, but he could not be sure. He was tired, hungry, and disoriented and looking at life with only one eye. The lost soul had no idea where he was or where he was going. He just wanted to go home. He walked for hours, his cuts and bites inflicted by the wild dogs now stinging him every time he moved. He was moving slower and slower as the sun set yet again on another day.

The next morning a small country convenience store was opening for business, and a trash truck lifted the dumpster high in the air to dump its trash. He saw food scraps fall to the ground and he ran to them, pain shooting through his paws as he was chased away by the store manager cleaning up outside. But he had his prize, a half-eaten sandwich covered with ants, but it was food. Cars went whizzing by on the road nearby. Some threw trash along the roadside, which he chased in hopes of another meal.

Night was coming upon him again. He walked still looking and sniffing for food. He never had been this hungry before. His stomach was empty, his paws sore and bleeding and he was alone. The young puppy dreamt of home and the playful kids he watched over every day, his warm blanket on the floor in the corner by the fireplace and the sounds of laughter throughout the house. He dreamed of the fresh meat from his food bowl and the plentiful table scraps they all bestowed upon him including the parents... he missed home.

He sniffed the air and found a familiar smell, he smelled friends. He sniffed again and followed the trail. Walking down a dark country road, he tread in the grass stopping many times to lick his paws.

He was tired, very tired, when he saw a big white house at the end of the lane with another larger green building not far away with a fence completely encircling it. The scent was coming from the larger building and now he could hear some barking noises coming from the larger building. They were good sounds, food sounds, contented food sounds.

Stopping, he could go no further. He lay down to rest by the mailbox in front of the house. The mailbox sported a cutout of a large dog at the top and the name Hidden Valley Dog Shelter appeared on the side with the name Dr. Marion Summers, Veterinarian underneath. He lifted himself up and trudged towards the house, finally settling at the base of the steps and let out a loud whine. He could go no further.

*Doc Marion,* as everyone called her, finished the dishes in her kitchen, and turned out the lights, preparing to cuddle in bed with her half-finished Danielle Steele novel. It had been a long tiring day.

She poured herself a glass of port and with her book under one arm and her sleeping potion in the other she headed for the stairs. She made it to the third step when she heard a cry outside for help.

She stopped and heard it again. It was unmistakable. She turned on the outside porch light and saw the battered puppy lying at the foot of her porch. "You poor dear," she said setting down her book and glass of wine and rushed to his side. Danielle Steele would have to wait.

Doc patted his head to tell him she was of the friendly sort and talked to him with her soft reassuring voice. She knelt down in front of him, stroking his head, "Hmm, no collar? Another dog with no name, huh puppy? Did someone leave you out on the road to be found by farmers? Lucky you weren't eaten by the wild dogs around here. Although look at you. No matter, you're home now. Come on, let's go fix you up and get you something to eat." He made a feeble attempt to lick her to show his gratitude.

The vet lifted him ever so gently, but he still yelped in pain. She felt his pain in her chest, as she carried him to her office and walked to the kennel building. All the other dogs barked when she opened the door to the kennel, and the black lab could tell they were all greeting barks. They were happy to see her. Doc walked by the pens, greeting each one by name when she went past.

She opened the door to her office and laid him on the examining table. "Let's have a look at that eye," she said to him while setting him down softly. She cleansed the blood from the now swollen eye and applied a compress. "That should heal nicely," she told him in an encouraging voice, holding him under his jaw, touching noses. "You must have thought you were blind in one eye, huh? Yeah, I know how you feel."

She examined him thoroughly, dressing his other wounds while he lapped cool water down his parched throat. Doc Marion retrieved some food from the nearby cupboard and had him eat but only a little at a time. He responded to her gentle but firm touch, by licking her face and hand in appreciation.

"You must have some story to tell my unnamed new friend," she said to the now recovering overgrown puppy. He cocked his head telling her he understood what she was asking while continuing to lick her hand in thanks.

"We need to get you to a place where you can rest, you big lug. Come on. Can you sit up?" He tried to rise but collapsed in a heap on the examining table.

"Okay. You want to be carried. Is that it?" He cocked his head again but did not move.

She put her arm underneath the large lab puppy and picked him up, carrying him to the holding area reserved for new arrivals. "You are a heavy puppy," she told him with a smile, which soon turned to *an aching look on her face, the sharp pain stilled her heart.*

*She gasped, Susan, Susan,* she cried to herself in agony, her last thoughts, she *would never see her beautiful daughter Susan again,* the pain now unbearable from her breaking heart.

She fell to the floor, and the puppy lost his newfound friend. Dr. Marion Summers was dead by the time she hit the floor, her last act on this earth, was one of gentle kindness to a stray dog again a dog with no name. He licked her face before he scurried to the corner, scared and shivering. He was alone again.

# My Extraordinary Night with Frank

It was late, and I had been walking for what seemed like hours. All the stores and quaint little tourist shops were closed and shuttered.

I had rushed out of the hotel after I said some things in anger, but I couldn't go back now... he was there. I was lost, but I kept walking. *What was the name of the hotel again? Pensione something, something, something.* My feet hurt, and my ankles began to swell. I rubbed my swollen belly, and I wished he was here to rub my feet. I had to sit down.

City residents had piled the trash high along the streets of Rome, awaiting the early morning pickup by the trash men. The street cleaners were busy with their machines to begin their nightly ritual along the *Piazza del Risorgimento*. Down the street, I could see a light on inside a coffee shop. The sign on the awning said simply *De' Ris Café*.

An old man with frosty white hair, a green beret, and worn khakis sat out front at one of the many gleaming metal tables that lined the street. He sipped his espresso, intent on reading his newspaper. He looked up with a kind smile as I sat down and nodded in acknowledgement before returning to his paper.

It felt so good to sit down. I looked around, and seeing no one, I slipped off my shoes and began rubbing my swollen feet. He did it so much better... but he wasn't here.

A tired-looking waiter approached me with indifference, spouting a steady stream of Italian, none of which I understood.

"I don't speak Italian, I'm sorry," I tried to tell him but to no avail.

He continued his questions in an unfamiliar tongue.

"No speaka Italiano," I stammered again, but it was no use as he continued his blabbering monologue. He glanced down with disdain at my unsheathed feet, now resting comfortably on top of my old sneakers.

"I'm so sorry but I don't understand one word of ..."

"*Excusi, Signora,*" said the old gentleman at the nearby table. "American?" he asked in a voice just above a whisper, which immediately silenced the imposing waiter.

"No, I'm Canadian. Toronto." I took in a deep breath. My stomach twitched, hard. *Please God, don't let me have this baby now. What am I thinking? This can't be. I'm only...*

"Can I be of assistance?" the kind old man asked politely.

"I just want to sit down. I had a fight with my husband and left the hotel, and now I'm lost." *Why am I confessing all of this to him? I don't know why, maybe because he has my father's eyes, those kind, gentle eyes.*

"I just wanted to sit down, that's all."

"I think he wants you to order something. *Si?*" The waiter nodded his head in agreement without knowing why.

"All right then, tell him I'll have a coffee…an espresso. Thank you."

Minutes later the waiter returned with a small white cup of dark black coffee, one that was favored by the locals. It tasted bitter, but I drank it slow in order to maximize my time to sit and rub my feet. As I finished my coffee, the lights of the café went out behind me, and the waiter reappeared with the bill. I reached for my purse and realized I had left in such a hurry that I had neglected to bring it with me. Now not only was I tired, but I was also lost. I didn't remember the name of my hotel and I had no money. I was surely going to end up in jail as a thief, a vagrant, or a missing person, or all of the above. *How long would I be in jail?*

The neighborhood appeared safe, but a group of young men had just walked by earlier and looked strangely at me. I could still see them as they lingered at the intersection down the street.

*Now what?* I searched for some change, coins, crumbled old bills… anything. Nothing. Then I began to cry.

The old man beckoned for the server. He reached inside his pants pocket and procured several coins that he patiently counted out into the heavyset waiter's outstretched hands.

"*Grazie, patron*," he said, turned, and went back inside the café.

The old man stood, grabbed his walking cane from a nearby chair, and moved towards me.

"*Signora*, my car is here," he raised his cane and pointed to an old Renault. "It is too late for taxis this evening, but if you will allow me… I can give you a ride back to your hotel."

I stopped crying long enough to answer, "I don't know the name of the hotel or where it is in Rome." My tears began again.

"*Signora*," he said as he held out his hand, "come with me." I was a big-city girl but no alarm bells went off in my head, no red flags, and no hesitation, the only thing I felt was… trust. I took his hand, as he helped me stand. It was smooth and warm, like that of a surgeon or a writer. I followed where he led.

We stopped at the Renault, and he opened the door and helped me into the front seat. "Nice car," I whispered to myself. He heard me.

"How old are you?" he asked.

"I just turned thirty last month."

"Ah, same age as my car but both of you are in pretty good shape wouldn't you agree. Si?"

I had to laugh. *Who was this man?*

"What is your name?" I asked him as he tried to start the thirty-year-old relic of a car.

"You can call me Frank."

It took three times turning the key in the ignition before the car responded. He shifted the gears multiple times before it moved away from the curb onto the darkened street.

*I can't believe I am doing this. In Rome at two A.M., without Jerry, in a car with a strange… but nice old man… riding to God knows where. What was I thinking? He could be a mass murderer. Quick. Better say a prayer, dummy. No say two prayers! Ah, but it does feel good to sit down.*

The tiny car moved down the street, and he drove onto the Piazza towards the Vatican. He drove past the main Vatican entrance, down a side street, onto an alley before he entered a small gateway. A Swiss guard looked at him as he slowed the old car. The guard waved him through. *Well that's a relief. At least somebody knows him.* I began to relax. The old man had a very calming effect.

He stopped the car outside a small cottage on *Via Santa Marta*, that even in the moonlight I could see was badly in need of painting and obviously had seen better days. The same could be said of most of the buildings in Rome, but I loved it since it only seemed to add to their quaint charm and character. The numbers 201 hung above the door with the number two dangling upside down. "I keep meaning to fix that," he said as he noticed my observant eye.

He pushed the ancient oak door, which was unlocked, and once inside he turned on a dim wall light to reveal a tiny apartment.

"Please come in," he said as a green and white Italian *Polizei* sedan drove by slowly and parked outside near the curb. The car headlights went dim.

I was tired and my feet were beginning to ache again. I needed to sit down, quickly. The pain in my belly twitched once more, this time only sharper and longer. *No God please, not again. Not again, please.*

It was as if he knew what I needed, "Sit down here, and let me get you a glass of water. Then I will make us some tea."

As I sat, I looked around the small apartment. It was clean but very simple. A small wooden desk with a pile of papers neatly stacked on top sat next to an old rotary telephone. One red rose sat in a half-filled jar of water. A small cot was off to the left, with neatly folded white sheets covering a thin mattress. A crucifix hung over the bed. In the adjacent room was a kitchen table with two chairs and a small kitchenette.

Above me on the wall was a picture of Pope John XXIII, a crucifix, and picture of Saint Joseph and Mary. On the wall by his desk, I could see a picture of the San Lorenzo soccer team with the flag of Argentina flying behind them. Four books adorned a small shelf next to his chair, the Holy Bible, *Das Capital* by Karl Marx, *The Holy Writings of Saint Francis of Assisi*, and *Crime and Punishment* by Dostoyevsky.

"Here my dear," he said handing me a glass of water. The water was cool and sweet, like that from a fresh well. It was refreshing and seemed to help. *Who was this man?*

He handed me a pencil and piece of paper, "Would you please write down your name and home address? I will see what I can do to help reunite you with your husband." My stomach soured again, emitting a sharp pain. I clutched my belly.

"Are you all right, my child?" he asked.

"I lost my last baby three years ago during a very difficult childbirth. The doctors said I should never try again, but I wanted a child more than anything. My husband is very concerned about me since I nearly died during my last pregnancy. He has suggested alternatives ... maybe he's right. We had a big fight about it tonight, and I left angry at him. I love him, and I want a baby. But now I'm thinking that maybe he's right. I'm so ashamed." *Why am I telling this man all of this? What manner of man is this?* A pain shot through my stomach and up through my chest. I held my belly tight and grimaced.

The kind old man lowered his hand and gently passed it over my large protruding stomach, "You will be fine my dear, just fine," he whispered in a reassuring voice. He was right... the pain immediately went away and didn't returned.

He walked to the door and met with a uniformed guard whom he handed the paper to, the one that contained my name and address. After they exchanged a few words in Italian, the young guard was gone.

We talked for what must have been hours or rather I talked and he listened, nodding at times, smiling at others. I told him about my family, my job, my dreams, my husband, my politics, and my religion,

He was very easy to talk to, much easier than most. He made a pot of tea as I sat on the chair in the small kitchen.

I finally looked at him and asked, "Who are you?"

He smiled that now familiar smile, paused, and said, "I am just a sinner."

"No… I mean…, what do you do?"

He paused again to reflect before answering, "I am a caretaker. When is your baby due?" he asked changing the subject and poured me yet another cup of tea.

"I'm due the same month as my birthday—December."

"Ah, that's a good month for a birthday. My birthday is also in December… the 17th. He will be a fine healthy boy, no doubt."

*How did he know I was expecting a boy?*

He smiled again. I noticed another bible was open on a nearby side table.

"Do you pray a lot… sir?"

His eyes smiled a genteel smile. "Yes, I do…all the time."

"Are you praying now?"

"Every moment of life is a prayer…but you knew that already didn't you, my dear?"

He could see right through me and knew just what I was thinking, much as my father did when I was a child growing up in Winnipeg. I felt exposed and ashamed before him. "I don't know what you mean father," I stammered.

He smiled, "Come have some more tea. Breakfast will be here soon."

The kitchenette was small with a crucifix over the rear door that led out to a small garden, visible now in the growing morning light. "You know the right thing to do. The challenge now for you and your family is to do it. But it is up to you," he said calmly pouring my tea and sliding a small tray of sugar cubes to rest in front of me.

*Who is this man?*

There was a knock at the door and an old woman dressed in black walked inside carrying a breakfast tray of fruit, toast, yogurt, and some juice accompanied by two plates. She did not seem the least bit surprised to find me there, alone with the white-haired old man. She set the tray on the table, nodded good morning to both of us, and left as quietly as she had arrived.

The fruit was fresh, and the yogurt was the sweetest I had ever tasted. We ate in silence, then he looked at me and began to talk. "My dear, life is full of crossroads. Most of life's most difficult challenges are ones that we did not ask for, but they also make us the strongest. You have choices to make, but I am sure you will make the best choice you can and you will be a stronger person for it. I will pray for you, for your family because I feel…" a soft knock on the door interrupted him. A uniformed guard entered and whispered something in his ear. He bowed and smiled at me as he left.

"Your ride back to your hotel is here."

"How did they find out where I was staying? Who are you?"

I noticed his ornate gold ring when he extended his hand to me, "Come now, you must be tired, and I am sure your husband is worried about you. The police car will take you to him." As he walked me to the door he said, "Thank you for sharing your thoughts and your time with me. I will pray for you and for your son," and he held out his hand for me to shake. Instinctively I kissed his ring, and thanked him.

Jerry was so happy to see me, and he didn't even yell at me for my misadventures with my new friend Frank. He just looked at me strangely. We talked for hours and we had lunch on the *Piazza d' Roma*. I love him more than anything in the world. Finally, we talked about names for the baby and I told him I had a favorite if it was a boy.

"I thought you wanted a girl?"

"You never know what life may bring you." I told him with a smile as I held his hand as we walked past the art galleries near the Vatican.

We spent two extra days in Rome, and wandered through the Vatican learning all about it …we learned a lot. After that day, I finally knew the answer to the question that I had asked myself many times that night, that night in Rome, Who was that man?

When the baby was born, some months later, it was a boy. We named him Francis. Later in life, when I told my son that this was a true story, his eyes showed his disbelief. However, every year in December, he would receive a card in the mail from Rome. It would be in a small gold envelope. The flap was closed with an official-looking red wax seal, and inside would be the careful hand-scripted words:

*Happy Birthday*

*Frank*

# Breakfast

*This is not rain,* I thought, *this is a flood!* Our SUV had chosen this day to quit, stranding me halfway to work, in the torrential rain, with the BMW dealership and AAA telling me there was a four-hour wait for service.

My husband, Paul, had commandeered my sedan that morning and headed in the opposite direction to take the kids to school.

The office was not yet open, and the ironically named Sunshine Cab Company, informed me, "Lady, everybody wants a taxi today in this rain," which left me with one last option to get to work—the bus.

Paul was dry, I thought to myself, and I was soaking wet and stuck; now having to resort to riding the bus. *Damn him*, I thought to myself. He must have had a premonition about the car that morning. *He always had the good luck, not me. Well, the car needed gas, so he'll have to get wet like me to get it filled up. Serves him right.*

I grabbed my briefcase and umbrella from the back seat of the SUV and ran the three blocks in heels to the bus stop, my skirt, and new shoes getting drenched in the process. I was glad the bus stop was sheltered and when I arrived there, I found two old men filling the bench in the only dry place for blocks around.

"Good morning," I muttered.

"Mornin'," they both responded. They looked in my direction. The one nearest to me wore an oversized olive wool overcoat, still wet from the rain. He sported a tired, soaked Yankees baseball cap. The other older man had large sad eyes, rimmed with wild bushy grey eyebrows. His faded blue tie had a grease stain in the center and one of his shirt collars was riding high over his ragged tan raincoat.

"Can I catch the bus to downtown here?" I asked, as the rain continued to pour outside, forming huge puddles in the street.

"Yes, you can. All the buses stop here. Look for one that says Downtown—Charles Center on the front."

"Thanks. My husband took the car today, and mine broke down just up the road, so I'm stuck taking the bus," I told them looking to make conversation.

The nearest man in the green overcoat looked up and said, "Well ma'am, I don't have a car, and my friend Wilson here, just lost his wife, his wife of fifty-eight years."

Now humbled and ashamed of myself for complaining, I scrambled and said to the older one, "I am so sorry for your loss. Please accept my condolences."

They both looked at me, their pleading eyes begging for more. *But what more could a stranger say?* Their eyes continued to ask questions without saying a word.

I stumbled and searched for something further to say, finally asking, "And what do you miss the most now that she's gone?"

Old Wilson took a deep breath and looked away for a brief moment before saying, "Now that she's gone… I don't have anyone to fight with anymore." Their bus stopped in front of the bus shelter and the doors opened.

"Here's our ride. We're going for breakfast, the best meal of the day. Nice talking to you, ma'am. Have a good day."

Watching the bus pull away, feeling so alone, I reached for my cell phone and called Paul, "Hey babe, wanna join me for some coffee and breakfast?"

---

Dear Reader—

I hope you enjoyed this selection of short stories. As a writer, I love to write probably as much as you love to read. Short stories are truly like a box of chocolates, you never know what you are going to find. If you enjoyed them, my other novels are listed below. Thanks again for your support. It means a lot. Look for my upcoming books wherever fine books are sold.

*Bryan Mooney*

A Box of Chocolates

Love Letters

A Second Chance

The Potus Papers

INDIE—A Female Vigilante